'Do you know a special way for calming babies, Alex?' She sighed as the child cried in her arms.

'Noisy babies are universal. As is the way of calming them.'

Carly could see the joy in Alex's eyes as he said, 'I should love to try.'

He held baby Esme with such care and tenderness. He walked her up and down, rocking her gently with obvious expertise. But he couldn't stop that tiny wail.

Carly smiled. 'What are you going to do now? What else would you do in Russia?'

'Sing to her,' said Alex.

'Well, go on, then. Sing to her.' Alex looked round, and she saw that he was seriously thinking about it. 'If you want to, that is,' she added.

'Very well,' said Alex.

He started to sing quietly, trying to lull the baby to sleep. And his voice was as soft, as seductive as anything Carly had ever heard. He might be trying to make the baby sleep. But to Carly the sounds conjured up quite a different scene. This was a love song. And she felt that Alex was singing it to her.

Dear Reader

A year ago I wrote three books—A VERY SPECIAL MIDWIFE, A CHILD TO CALL HER OWN, and THE NOBLE DOCTOR. They were about life in a maternity unit in a large city hospital, the Dell Owen. I was really pleased at the number of letters I received saying how much readers had enjoyed the Dell Owen trilogy, and asking was there any chance of any more? No need to ask; I love writing about maternity. So now we have another three.

My daughter is a midwife. She supplies me with the technical details for my stories, and the feelings that nurses, doctors, midwives have about their profession. They are trained not to let their feelings show—but they are there, especially in a life-enhancing department like Maternity.

These latest three books are about two brothers and a sister, all working together in the Dell Owen Hospital. Jack, Toby and Carly are vastly different in character, united in their love for each other, but feel that sibling rivalry that is a part of so many high-achieving families. All three fall in love—though *the course of true love never did run smooth'*.

I hope you get as much pleasure from reading about the Dell Owen Hospital staff as I get from writing about them.

With all good wishes

Gill Sanderson

A BABY OF
THEIR OWN

BY
GILL SANDERSON

MILLS & BOON®
Pure reading pleasure

First published in Great Britain 2007
Large Print edition 2007
Harlequin Mills & Boon Limited,
Eton House, 18-24 Paradise Road,
Richmond, Surrey TW9 1SR

© Gill Sanderson 2007

ISBN: 978 0 263 19377 0

Set in Times Roman 16½ on 19 pt.
17-1207-48505

Printed and bound in Great Britain
by Antony Rowe Ltd, Chippenham, Wiltshire

Gill Sanderson, aka Roger Sanderson, started writing as a husband-and-wife team. At first Gill created the storyline, characters and background, asking Roger to help with the actual writing. But her job became more and more time-consuming and he took over all of the work. He loves it!

Roger has written many Medical™ Romance books for Harlequin Mills & Boon®. Ideas come from three of his children—Helen is a midwife, Adam a health visitor, Mark a consultant oncologist. Weekdays are for work; weekends find Roger walking in the Lake District or Wales.

Recent titles by the same author:

THE DOCTOR'S BABY SURPRISE*
A SURGEON, A MIDWIFE: A FAMILY*
A NURSE WORTH WAITING FOR
TELL ME YOU LOVE ME
THE NOBLE DOCTOR*
A CHILD TO CALL HER OWN*
A VERY SPECIAL MIDWIFE*

Dell Owen Maternity

For the Inman sisters:
Nellie, Minnie, Esme and Cathleen.

Much missed.

CHAPTER ONE

THE man strode into the Delivery Room, nodded briefly at Carly and at Nancy Roberts, the midwife, and went straight to their near-exhausted patient, placing a hand on her forehead. His voice was deep as he bent over the woman and whispered, *'Kak pozhivaesh?'*

It made no sense to Carly but it obviously meant something to their patient. For the first time she managed to smile. She grabbed the man's hand and replied with a torrent of words that still made no sense to either Carly or Nancy. But the man understood. He nodded and whispered back a few words in the same soothing tone.

'Are you the husband of this woman? There are a few questions we'd like to ask you.' Nancy's voice was cold. She was the midwife, this was her Delivery Room. Strangers did not just walk into it unannounced.

The man straightened, looked at Carly and Nancy with flashing dark eyes. 'I am not this woman's husband; I have never seen her before. I heard a cry for help and I came to answer it.'

Carly sighed to herself. She saw that Nancy was not very pleased with this answer. This could turn into a full-scale row—which was the last thing that was needed in a Delivery Room with a lonely mum-to-be who spoke no English. So it was up to Carly to smooth things over. Well, all part of a junior registrar's job.

'We're having a bit of trouble here,' she said, 'and we'd appreciate any help you can give. This lady is an emergency patient. Apparently she started labour early while she was on the InterCity train; the crew called ahead for an ambulance and she was brought straight here. But we don't know who she is or anything about her medical history. And all we can get out of her is that her name is Katya. We don't even know what language she is speaking.'

'She is speaking Russian. And of course I will help you with the birth; I am a doctor.' He looked at the two unimpressed faces staring at him. 'That is,' he said after a pause, 'I would like to act as…as an advisor and perhaps a translator if you feel the patient would be happier that way. Perhaps I could…'

This was too much. As courteously as she could manage, Carly said, 'The patient already has a doctor. Me. And I shall remain doctor in charge until ordered to do otherwise by one of my clinical superiors. First, though, I want to know who you are and whether you really are a doctor or not. Will you wait outside until I find out?'

'Like I said, I am a doctor, and my name is Alex Braikovitch. And I think your patient could do with my help.'

'I'll phone Security,' Nancy said. 'They'll throw you out on your neck.' She made her way to the internal telephone.

The man looked at her calmly. 'I will wait outside,' he said, 'but I do feel that this woman needs me and that I could help both you and her.

Ring John Bennett and tell him that Dr Alex Braikovitch is here. I could be needed and I'm offering to help.'

Nancy looked at Carly, who said, 'I'll phone him. Dr Braikovitch, if you'd leave now…?'

There was time for one thoughtful glance. The man bent over the patient, whispered to her again, and then walked out.

'I suspect he'll be back,' Nancy said when the door had closed behind him. 'He seems a determined type.' Then she smiled and shook her head at the patient, who had just burst out with another speech in what they now knew to be Russian. 'He's quite something too.'

Fortunately John Bennett, the head of Obs and Gynae, was in his office. Carly explained the situation and John laughed. 'Alex is here? I wasn't expecting him till the end of the week. Typical of the man to turn up early. Look, I'll explain all about him later. I'll be down to collect him in a while but if you can use him before then, then do so. You'll find he's one of the world's workers. He's here to teach us a few things,

Carly, but perhaps we can teach him a few things too.'

'Right,' Carly said, replacing the receiver. She had thought of asking John if they were to teach this man what was protocol in the Delivery Room—but then decided not to do so. If John approved of him, then there must be some good in him. Somewhere.

From behind her came another frightened outburst from their patient. And there was no way that either she or Nancy could reply. Carly felt a slight twinge of guilt; she knew that when a woman was having her first baby, just how important it was to have her partner or mother with her. Katya had no one, not even someone who spoke her language. She must be feeling so lonely.

'John says he's a doctor; he can come in if you want him,' she said to Nancy. 'John says he's all right.'

'If Katya here wants him, then I want him too,' said Nancy. 'This must be a desolate birth for her so far. But we're still in charge.'

'Of course. I'll get him in.'

Carly went to the door, opened it. 'Dr Braikovitch, you've been vouched for; we'd appreciate your help.'

The man nodded, followed her back into the Delivery Room. Carly went on, 'We think the baby is about a month premature, but so far there have been no adverse signs. This should be a perfectly straightforward birth. We're now well into the second stage and we're quite confident about the delivery.'

'Do you wish me to deliver the baby?'

'No. What we'd like you to do is comfort the patient, translate any instructions we have for her. And we'd also like to know a little bit about her—is there anything in her medical history that we should know, anyone we ought to inform? We've looked through the little bag she was carrying, there's no information there.'

'I see.'

'Would you like any kind of protective clothing?'

'Since I don't seem to be taking any very active part in these proceedings, then I don't think it necessary.'

'Quite,' said Carly. 'Incidentally, this is Midwife Nancy Roberts; I am Dr Carly Sinclair.'

'We can't shake hands,' Nancy said, waving rubber-gloved fingers at him.

'Perhaps later.' He bowed to them, a gentle inclination of the head that Carly found very graceful. 'I am very pleased to meet you both.'

Even though he was speaking to them both, Carly noted that his eyes constantly flicked to the patient on the bed. Now he moved to stand by her head again, took a cloth and wiped her sweat-beaded forehead. He spoke to her, his deep voice much more gentle than it had been. She reached for his hand, gripped it and spoke back to him. Alex nodded.

'This lady is Katya Semenov. She thanks you for what you have done for her so far and says she could not be in better hands. She is sorry she speaks no English.'

'I think she knows what pant and push mean now,' Nancy commented. 'And she knows how to breathe.'

Alex moved down a little, looked at what Nancy was doing. 'Fully dilated? And all well? Head at the spine?'

Carly nodded. 'Tell her that it won't be long now. Can you find out something about her husband? About what she's doing here?'

'Of course.' There was a quick exchange of words and then Alex said, 'Katya flew from Moscow and was on her way to meet her husband who's a visiting lecturer in Glasgow University. She says he'll be worried about her; he was going to meet her off the train. The baby was not expected for another month.'

There was a snort from Nancy. 'Babies tend to pick their own time of arrival.'

'I agree with you. But I would like to try to get in touch with Katya's husband, tell him where she is and that she is being well looked after. I am sure he'll be here quite quickly.'

'Use that telephone and ask for an outside line,' Carly said. 'If you can get through to her husband, tell him Katya will phone him as soon as she's got some good news.'

'Right.' Alex moved to the phone. At first he spoke in English, but after a while Carly heard him speaking in the musical tongue he had used with Katya. It was just possible to guess what he was saying. At first there were the formal questions to establish identity and then the slightly louder calming, reassuring tones that meant that his listener was worried. Finally he rang off.

Alex went back to Katya, smoothed her hair and spoke to her again. There was a rapid excited exchange and then an undeniable gasp of pain.

'Not long now,' Nancy announced. She looked up to see Alex moving towards her. 'We can cope quite well down here, Doctor,' she said. 'Your job is to help the mother.'

Carly had to hide her smile. Alex was obviously a hands-on doctor. He didn't like being kept out of things.

After that things went normally, perfectly, just as they were intended to do. Half an hour later the baby was born, Nancy as midwife, Carly on take. 'And it's a little girl!' Nancy announced.

She clamped and cut the cord as, like a deeper

echo, Alex's voice came back as he translated. *'Mahlyinkaya dyevooshka Katya.'*

Carly made a quick check for the Apgar scale, then dried and wrapped the baby in a towel. After the first tiny yell, Nancy gave an injection of one ml of syntometrine, to expedite the delivery of the placenta and reduce the risk of bleeding. Carly went to hand the baby to her mother.

Alex was facing her, his hands outstretched. 'May I give her to her mother?' he asked.

In fact it was something that Carly rather enjoyed doing, but she supposed that it would be better for the mother if Alex did it. She handed over the baby. Then looked in horror.

Alex took the baby, smiled at her and showed her to her mother. *'Tvoi mladenec.'* Then, instead of tucking the baby to her mother's breast, with two hands he lifted the infant high over his head, gazing up at her. *'Ti takaya krasivaya,'* he called. And only then did he hand the baby to her smiling, weeping mother.

A furious Carly pulled Alex aside. 'Dr Braikovitch, that was stupid and dangerous!'

she muttered fiercely. 'What did you think you were doing?'

Alex didn't seem at all contrite. 'I told a newborn little girl that she was beautiful,' he said. 'And I lifted her to Heaven because she is Heaven's gift to her mother.' Then his voice became more formal. 'It is an old custom in the part of Russia where Katya was born. She feels alone here, away from her family, her friends, her husband. I lifted the child to make her feel, just a little, at home.'

'Just so long as you didn't drop her,' Nancy put in.

Now his voice was mild. 'I have held many babies and it is something I like doing. And I have yet to drop one.'

Carly wondered if she had overreacted. 'Sorry,' she conceded. 'It was just a bit of a surprise.'

'Quite so. And it is I who should be sorry.'

Like all brand-new mothers, Katya was now engrossed with her baby. She bared her breast, eased it towards the tiny toothless mouth, watched fascinated as it tried to fasten on the nipple. An equally tiny hand came from the towel, waved bravely at the new world outside.

It was a sight that Carly loved, could never tire of. And, as she looked at the grey-suited figure opposite her, she realised that he felt exactly the same.

The job was now nearly finished. A success-ful birth, a happy mother and a healthy baby, a husband on his way. There was no need to worry further. Nancy would be more than capable of finishing what was left to do. Now she could pay some attention to the man who had entered— well, if not her life, then her Delivery Room. So she looked at him, perhaps properly for the first time.

And her world rocked.

So far he had been little more than a man in a dark grey suit, white shirt, some nondescript tie or other. She knew he was tall, broad-shouldered, had black hair. The most attractive thing about him she had noticed had been his voice. It was deep. He spoke English perfectly, with perhaps a little more precision than a native-born speaker. But when he spoke his own language, the sound was like music.

Nothing really special—she knew many men fitting this description. So why was her heart beating faster, lurching within her breast? Why was she breathing so quickly, why was her brow so suddenly warm? This had never happened to her before!

She stared at him, hypnotised by his grey-blue eyes, as piercing as sun on Siberian snow. She had never met a man like this, had never felt like this in anyone's presence. Why should she now?

He wasn't tremendously handsome. There was little that was rounded or soft in his face; it was a mixture of planes and angles. Her brother Jack was supposed to have a craggy face, this one was even craggier. High wide cheek bones, eyebrows like rock, a strong forehead. The only concession to warmth or kindness was his mouth. That was wide, the lips sometimes curving when he smiled. When he smiled there was a hint of a different person. But he didn't seem to smile very often.

Then she realised two things. First, that she was staring at him. Second, that he was staring back at her. Their glances met, fused; it was impossible for her to look away. And there was a moment of communion; she knew with absolute certainty that he felt the same as she did. But they had only just met!

Neither could speak—not with words. Their trance had to be broken by someone else. Dimly Carly registered that the door to the Delivery Room had been opened, that someone had entered. A cheerful voice said, 'Nancy, all right if I come in?'

'Of course,' said the midwife. 'We appear to be having a party here.'

There was a laugh and then the voice went on, 'Alex, it's good to see you. Just like you—busy already.'

Carly saw the spark of recognition dying in Alex's eyes, registered the wariness that returned. They were back in the real world. She knew that her own face would be showing the same change to cautious neutrality. And they

both turned to meet John Bennett, Carly's imme-
diate boss, the Obs and Gynae Consultant.

'John, it is good to see you again too.' Carly
watched as the two men shook hands, and then
blinked as Alex folded John in a bear hug and
lifted him off the ground. She managed to hide a
smile as she glimpsed John's expression of slight
alarm. Obviously things were different in Russia.

'I gather you've met Dr Sinclair here. She's
one of my junior registrars; she's on the fast
track to be promoted.'

'I have watched her work; she is very impressive. I hope I may work with her in the future.'

John looked at her speculatively. 'Is that so?
Well, that's good. I'm already planning to timetable you together.'

This was news to Carly. 'My life seems to be
being arranged for me,' she pointed out, 'and
I'm not even being consulted. John, I don't even
know what Dr…Dr…'

'Braikovitch,' the man supplied. 'But I hope
you will call me Alex, and you are…'

'Carly. Carly Sinclair.'

They shook hands and she wondered if he felt the same throb of excitement that she did as her skin touched his. But now she couldn't tell from his face; it was impassive.

She had to keep her head; she was a cool, careful doctor. Well, she could be. She went on, 'John, I don't really know what Dr Braikovitch—Alex—is doing here. No new posts have been advertised.'

John smiled. 'Alex here is not to be a proper member of staff but he'll have the rank of Senior Registrar. He's head of a small hospital in Russia; he's here just for three months, to work with us, specifically to offer us the benefit of his experience in dealing with infant and childhood infectious diseases.'

'I see,' said Carly, now looking at Alex with new, more appreciative eyes. 'In that case, Alex, I look forward to working with you.'

She knew that infectious diseases were on the increase again in Britain. With an increasingly mobile world population, diseases such as typhoid, tuberculosis, meningitis, diphtheria, even malaria were becoming much more common than they had been even twenty years ago. And knowledge about them was now rare and precious.

John went on, 'Alex's stay is being funded by a charity—MedAsia—Medicine in Asia. I'm one of the committee members. We've helped them in the past—they now want to help us.'

'I'm deeply grateful to John and to MedAsia for giving me this chance,' Alex's deep voice said. 'I'll be happy to teach—and I do hope to learn as well.'

'I hope you'll be happy with us, Alex,' she said. 'And I'm sure you'll be a good teacher. But why did you specialise in infectious diseases?'

His smile was brief. 'For centuries the land I live in has been the cockpit of Asia. It has been the crossroads for armies, for smugglers, for traders. They come, they go—and they leave their diseases behind. We've had to learn to deal with it.'

'You'll have plenty to teach us,' John said. He glanced at his watch. 'Look, Alex, I've got a meeting in five minutes; it's going to be an hour or so before I can talk to you. Your fault for coming early! Carly, what are you doing now?'

She shrugged. 'Not a lot for the moment. I've got notes to write up in the doctors' room. If Alex wants to come along there with me, he'll be more than welcome.' She looked at the man. 'Do you spend much time filling in medical forms in Russia, Alex?'

His reply was ironic. 'I spend too much time filling in forms, sending them to offices many miles away. And, I suspect like here, the forms seem to be ignored. I much prefer hands-on medicine.'

'Settled, then,' said John, obviously deciding not to get drawn into a conversation about the relative merits of form-filling in two countries. 'I'll see you both in the doctors' room in about an hour, then.' And he was gone.

Carly took Alex to the door of the Delivery Room, pointed down the broad corridor. 'I want to get out of these scrubs,' she said. 'If you walk to the corner, turn right, the third door on your left is the doctors' room. Introduce yourself to anyone who might be in there, but I don't think there will be. Help yourself to coffee or tea and I'll be with you in a moment.'

'Right,' he said, and set off at once.

Obviously not a man to waste time on unnecessary chatter, Carly thought. She watched him as he walked. He moved quickly, easily, like a man at ease in his own body. He reminded her of some wild animal—a wolf loping across icy plains. Do they still have wolves in Russia? she wondered. Perhaps she would ask him. Then she frowned. What was she thinking; this was stupid! He was just a colleague and she intended to maintain a professional distance, no matter how intriguing Alex was.

She had a quick shower, spent two minutes more than usual on her minimal make-up and re-arranging her hair. Then she went to talk to Dr Alex Braikovitch. She decided that she *was* curious about him and that there were a couple of things she had to put right.

That odd experience in the Delivery Room—well, it was just that. An odd experience. She was a scientist; she knew that it was impossible for feeling to flow between two people just because they were looking at each other. She hadn't had much sleep recently, the room had been necessarily warm. Perhaps she hadn't been quite herself, so she could forget the incident. Could she?

But it had seemed very real. More real than anything that had happened to her for quite some time.

He stood as she entered the doctors' room, bowed his head slightly. As she had thought—hoped—he was alone. They could chat in private.

There was a mug on the table in front of him. 'Good. Glad to see you got yourself some coffee,' she said.

He shook his head, lifted the mug so she could see and smell its contents. 'Black tea,' he said. 'Strong black tea—I needed two tea bags. Some doctors live on the caffeine from coffee; I am a

Russian, I live on the caffeine from tea.' He smiled. 'But there was no lemon.'

'I suspect you'll have to provide your own lemon.' She poured herself a mug from the ever-bubbling coffee pot, then waved at the collection of brightly coloured sachets of herbal teas. 'Nothing here interest you, then?'

'I am accustomed to herbs that are grown in gardens, not wrapped in paper. I think those might be a little weak.'

'Perhaps so.' She decided this conversation was getting nowhere. Who cared about tea, anyway? 'Alex, have you ever worked in a British hospital before?'

'Never. My original training was in Moscow; I have worked in hospitals there and in St Petersburg. For two separate six month periods I worked in hospitals in France—in Paris and Lyons.' He paused for a moment. Then, 'For the last seven years I have worked in a small hospital in a remote district that Russia and the rest of the world appears to have forgotten. I run the hospital and it's work that I love.'

'Run it? You are in complete charge?'

'We have three doctors. The other two are younger, they are hard-working, devoted to their jobs, desperate to learn, but largely untrained. I am older, more experienced. It would be unfair to saddle them with responsibilities they do not yet have the experience to deal with.'

There, she could feel it in his voice. The quiet confidence, the accepting of a job that might be hard but which had to be done. She asked, 'So you're basically an obs and gynae man?'

'And a paediatrician. And sometimes a surgeon as well as a clinician. Our hospital is supposed to cater for those specialities only. But the nearest general hospital is over a hundred miles away. So if anyone, of any age, needs urgent help—we do what we can for them.'

Carly winced. 'That must be a challenge. How do you cope?'

'We cope because we have to. There is no alternative.' He smiled. 'And I have to say that at times we quite enjoy it.' But underneath the smile she could detect something in his voice.

There was an utter determination to do what could be done—and then more.

For a moment she wondered what it would be like to work for, to train under Alex. Here, in the Dell Owen Hospital, John Bennett was her Consultant. His teaching style seemed casual at first; not a lot was forced on her, she was free to work at her own rate. The result, of course, was that she—and all the other junior doctors—worked like mad to learn and to impress him. She guessed it would be different working under Alex Braikovitch. He would expect everyone to give as he did. She wondered which teaching technique would be better. Certainly John's would be more pleasant. But working for Alex would be…stimulating?

She was daydreaming! And, as she looked up into his grey-blue eyes, she had the odd feeling that he had guessed what she was thinking. Ridiculous!

Time to change the subject. 'You're being supported while you're here by this charity, MedAsia,' she said. 'It sounds quite impressive.'

'It is. It has helped our work in the hospital considerably. And I am more than pleased that it has given us a chance to offer something back. I am looking forward to working with your infectious diseases unit.'

'I'm looking forward to it too,' she said honestly. 'There are things I need to know. I think I'm up to scratch on most of the work we have to do here—but infectious diseases are a bit of an unknown quantity. We don't see many but the number is growing.'

'I'm afraid so. Did John say that you were a junior registrar in obs and gynae?'

'I am. It's work I enjoy.'

'I thought I could tell that in the Delivery Room. And I gather we will be working together quite a lot?'

'That's quite possible.' She hoped he didn't detect the slight quaver in her voice as she spoke. The prospect of working with Alex Braikovitch was both exciting and alarming.

'I would like that,' he said.

A definite statement; she thought it meant

more than it said. Then there was another moment in which time seemed to stand still, in which they seemed to communicate without words or action.

He seemed more than content to remain silent. But she felt she had to speak; she had to establish what was between them. Or did she? Was she just imagining all of this? Eventually she muttered, 'Alex, it'll be nice to work with you but…'

Behind them, the door banged open. Carly jerked round and there was a smiling John Bennett.

'We finished early. Good of you to look after Alex for me in the meantime,' he told her.

'Not at all. We were having quite an interesting chat.' *Had it been more than a chat?*

'I'm glad. But now I'll take him off your hands. Alex, I've got papers for you to sign, people you have to meet, and I'll take you to the hospital flat where you're going to stay. Tomorrow you can start medicine proper.'

'I want to start as soon as possible,' Alex agreed.

'Well, first of all you need to know how we do things here. A sort of induction to the hospital before we start you off with responsibilities of your own. I'm working out a programme for you, but for a couple of days I'd like you to shadow one of our staff. Carly, do you mind if Alex works with you tomorrow?'

Her throat seemed suddenly dry, but she swallowed somehow and said, as coolly as possible, 'Not at all. I take it he is insured and he can be treated as a doctor?'

'Yes, of course,' said John. 'Well, that's settled, then. I think this will be a good experience for both of you.'

'I'm sure it will,' said Carly. She turned to look at Alex, whose face was entirely expressionless. 'Shall we meet here tomorrow morning? Say about eight?'

'I'm looking forward to it,' said Alex.

Carly loved her flat. It was small, but she had decorated it, furnished it, so it had everything she needed. It was her refuge, her comfort zone. Apart from her family, very few people were invited to visit here; she would rather meet them outside. Her brother Toby, in his typical cheerful, sometimes tactless way, had once said that she was womb recessive and this was the womb. Perhaps so. But if so, she was happy.

She followed her usual routine on coming back from hospital. First a bath or shower, then a complete change of clothes. Casual tonight; she wasn't going out again, so a pair of old jeans and a sweater.

And then a meal. Hurried eating was the curse of hospital doctors; too often her lunch was a chocolate bar or a sandwich, chewed while she walked from one ward to another. But at home she always ate with a tiny touch of style. This evening she sat at her table with a single glass of wine and enjoyed a cheese omelette and salad. Fruit afterwards. The dishes cleared away, she sat on the sofa to enjoy a coffee.

For a moment she looked round her living room. The family pictures on one wall. She shook her head; she suspected she'd soon have to find more space. Both her brothers now had children; there were two new photographs on the wall. And she knew there'd be more. What was lacking? Pictures of her own children? There seemed no chance of that at the moment. Not that she didn't want children. What she didn't want was a husband.

Her eye roved further. The single flower in the cut glass vase on her table. On the wall to her side, a glorious coloured Navajo rug, bought when she lived in Chicago. Her much-polished antique writing desk. All things that made her happy, made her feel comforted.

And then she sighed. She knew what she was doing—she was deliberately putting off thinking about Dr Alex Braikovitch. And Alex had to be thought about. He had disturbed her.

So what did she think of Alex? At first she hadn't liked him; she had thought him overbearing, somewhat arrogant, obviously accustomed to being the boss. But then she remembered the glow of delight in his eyes when he'd held Katya's new baby above his head. She remembered the concern he had for the labouring Katya herself. He was a caring and dedicated doctor.

She realised she was avoiding the issue. She was attracted to him, but she suspected he was not the kind of man for her. He was too dominant; in fact he was too male. But then she remembered those moments out of time in the Delivery Room, when her world had rocked, when the two of them had stared as if each could divine the other's thoughts. That had been magic, she had thought then. But now she was not so sure. Perhaps she had just been tired. Perhaps the whole thing had just been a momentary hallucination. That would make sense.

But she didn't think it had been a hallucination.

Then, perhaps inevitably, she thought of the man who had been the great love of her life. Dennis Clarkson. She had met him in Chicago when she had been studying at the Dana Hospital there. Dennis had been fun, exciting, the best-looking man she had ever met. She had thought she was the luckiest girl in the hospital, had been looking forward to a life of bliss with him. All her girl friends had envied her. And then she'd found out that he was married.

She had been sick with the horror of it, had had difficulty in carrying on with her course. And when, after much time, she did think that she was over him, she'd decided that men just weren't worth the risk. Men were all too much. She would stick to her career.

Alex was different, of course. She just couldn't imagine him keeping secrets from her; he was far too direct. He would say what he thought, without regard for the consequences.

Perhaps that made him an even greater risk than Dennis?

She made up her mind. There could be nothing between her and Dr Alex Braikovitch. The risk of pain was too great.

CHAPTER TWO

ALEX woke early. No matter how late he went to bed, he always woke early.

He was surprised; his first waking thought was of Carly. She had made something of an impression on him; there was something about her that... What was it?

He was sure he was beyond being drawn to someone just because they were physically attractive. Having said which, it had to be admitted that Carly *was* extremely attractive. She was tall, her figure was rounded—gracefully. Obviously no excessive slimming for Carly. Her hair was short, dark, neat—efficient for a busy doctor. Her eyes were large, blue; she had the habit of looking at him directly, as if defying him not to be honest with her.

This wasn't the way to think of her! He was cataloguing her, feature by feature, bit by bit, as if beauty could be defined like an order book for drugs. It wouldn't work.

Just an overall impression, then. She was beautiful. And her face reflected her feelings with an honesty that he found amazing. If she was angry, her cheeks flushed and her lips thinned. If she was happy—the smile on her face would tempt an angel.

Just the opposite to him! He knew it—he kept his feelings to himself. Things were easier that way.

What was he doing? He had work to do—no time to think now about beautiful women! With a ruthlessness that he had developed over the past few years, he thrust her from his mind. For now, at least.

He slipped on his dressing gown, wandered round the little flat allocated to him in the hospital grounds, looking at the washing machine, the central heating, the close-carpeted floors. Compared to what he had at home, this was luxurious.

He had stayed in Europe before, of course, had stayed in some of the more luxurious hotels. But a hotel was a place for an occasional visit. This flat was what a doctor might expect as his right. In fact, John had apologised for it being so small. Alex shrugged. He didn't need comfort to make him happy.

He showered—there was constant hot water! Then he made himself breakfast.

After showing him the flat yesterday, John had directed him to a supermarket near the hospital. Alex had walked over, bought himself some supplies. Now he prepared himself a typical English breakfast. Bacon and eggs! He wondered how long it would be before he reverted to the dishes he had at home. For breakfast he generally had sweet *plov*, a rice dish with dried apricots, raisins and prunes. He supposed he could make it here. But bacon and eggs was good.

He was meeting Carly at eight that morning so, after he'd washed the dishes, he set off to walk across the hospital grounds at seven. He always arrived early at his own hospital; it gave him time to look round, to see how things were progressing. He would rather make things happen than let them happen to him. But, since he was early, he thought he was entitled to think about Carly. In fact he was having difficulty in not thinking about her.

He was attracted to her—more than to anyone since he…well, since. Attracted to her? This was ridiculous. She was, he guessed, about twenty-seven or twenty-eight. He was thirty-five. But in life experience he was a hundred years older than her, not seven. In some ways he suspected she was still an innocent. They had so little in common; their views and experience of life were so different.

But he was still attracted to her. And he thought she was attracted to him. Yesterday, when their eyes had met in the Delivery Room, he had thought that… This was foolish! A quick physical attraction, that was all. Forget about it.

Using the code given to him by John yesterday, he entered the obs and gynae section. And as he walked he saw a figure he recognised—

surely that was the midwife he had met yesterday?

'Midwife Roberts—Nancy—I can see you are busy, but have you a moment?'

'Dr Braikovitch. Good morning.' Nancy's voice was polite, but distant.

'I think we can dispense with formality when we're not working,' he said, 'if you don't mind. Please call me Alex. The nurses in my own hospital do.'

It was the right thing to say. Nancy's entire attitude altered. She smiled at him, stopped, obviously happy to chat for a moment. 'Of course—Alex,' she said. 'You're in early.'

'I have a lot to learn before I can begin to teach. But first, how is Katya and her baby? I hoped yesterday to get in to see her, but it just wasn't possible. Perhaps later today, though.'

'Both doing well. And last night her husband turned up. He looked at his wife and his baby and he couldn't make up his mind whether to cry or be delighted. It was a joy to watch.'

'A family with a newborn baby is always a joy

to watch,' he said with a smile. 'Isn't that one reason why you became a midwife?'

'Well, yes. And I could tell you felt the same way when you held that baby over your head.' Nancy looked at him speculatively. 'What will you be doing today? Will we be seeing more of you? Will you hold more babies over your head?'

He laughed. 'I will hold babies over my head if the midwife will let me. Or perhaps it's a Russian custom I should leave in Russia. No, Nancy, this morning at least I'm shadowing Dr Sinclair—Carly, that is.'

'You'll do well with her. She's the Good,' Nancy said, then blushed. 'Sorry, that slipped out.'

But Alex was intrigued. 'You called her "the Good",' he said. 'What does that mean? Please, Nancy, I'm curious.'

Nancy blushed deeper. 'Just a daft nickname,' she said. 'You know she has two brothers, Jack and Toby, working in the hospital? Well, the three of them are called the Good, the Bad and the Ugly. You know, there's a film with that name.'

'I've seen it. Why are they called that?'

Now she'd got over her initial discomfort, Nancy was obviously enjoying herself. Alex thought that this was just like his own hospital; there was nothing like a good gossip. 'Well, Toby's the Bad. He's not really bad; he's settled down now and he's ever so happy. But he used to be… Do you know what "a bit of a lad" means?'

'I've come across the expression. What about Jack—the Ugly?'

'Well, he's not ugly—he's a lovely man. He's just a bit—a bit craggy. In fact he looks a bit like you.'

Alex grinned and wondered to himself if he had just been complimented or insulted. 'And Carly is called the Good?'

'If you work with her you'll find out why,' Nancy said. She glanced at her watch. 'Excuse me, work calls. Hope to see you later—Alex.' And she was gone.

Alex moved on down the corridor. So Carly was the Good in the Good, the Bad and the Ugly. He wanted to meet her two brothers now. If they were anything like Carly, then he thought he'd get on with them. But Carly...the Good?

He could see how it was suitable. She had the appearance of calm, of goodness. She was...sweet? No, that was the wrong word. He knew the words he needed in Russian. *Millaya moya.* A poor translation would be 'my sweet'.

But then his face grew grim. What was he thinking of? Emotions like this were not for him. He had to remember that.

It was a shock for Carly when she opened the door to the doctors' room and saw him for the first time since—since yesterday? It had seemed longer. This was odd, because—casually, of course—she had thought quite a lot about him over the past night.

It was almost like meeting someone new. He seemed bigger, more scary, more... All right, he seemed more sexy than he had yesterday. And she could feel that dryness in her throat again.

'I've brought you a white coat,' she told him, hoping her voice didn't croak. 'I hope it fits—it's the biggest size they had.'

'Thank you, Carly.' He took the coat from her. 'And I've got something for you to try. Were you going to have a coffee?'

'Of course. Like all doctors, I'm caffeine driven.'

'Then let me offer you an alternative. Perhaps, just for once.' He turned to the coffee table, flicked on the switch of the water heater. After a moment he handed her a mug. She took it suspiciously and smelled it.

'Black tea? With…with lemon?'

'Yesterday, in the large supermarket, I bought tea that was not in a bag and a store of fresh lemons.'

She sipped and pulled a face.

'You don't like it?' he asked.

She sipped again. 'Well, it's a bit of a shock; I was half expecting coffee.' She took another sip. 'You know, after a while it gets to be quite nice.'

'Like so many good things, it takes some getting used to. But I couldn't function without it. Now, the white coat.'

He pulled it on, wriggled inside it and eased the sleeves backwards. 'It has to fit; it's the largest size they have in stock,' she said, alarmed.

'It does fit. Look, here across the shoulders, under the arms. It couldn't fit better. The only thing is…' He pulled at the front of the coat. 'There is a little too much slack in the waist here. Are all your larger doctors fat?'

'Just leave it open,' she advised him. 'Go for the nonchalant look.' She knew as she said it that it was vain advice. Alex obviously didn't do nonchalant. He did committed.

'I shall take your advice. Now, where are you taking me? What are we to do? For today I will be your student, following you everywhere, taking notes on all that you tell me.'

'You don't look much like a student,' she told him. 'When I passed twenty-five I found that all student doctors looked incredibly young.'

She was glad that he didn't tell her she didn't look over twenty-five. 'Then I shall be what I am. A foreigner trying to understand the British way of doing things. And finding it very effective.'

'You'll go down well with the staff,' she told him, 'if you flatter like that. Come on, we'll start at an antenatal ward.'

He blinked. Him? A flatterer? What was happening to him?

There would be more time for a detailed look round later. But for now she showed him the full Delivery Suite: the admissions rooms, the antenatal wards, the delivery rooms, the postnatal wards, the transitional care ward, the special care baby unit and the antenatal clinic.

She noticed that he tried to remain impassive but he couldn't really manage it. After a while he shook his head. 'Something troubling you, Alex?'

'I'm envious,' he said gloomily. 'Of course, I have read all about the latest developments in obs and gynae care, and I have worked in good hospitals in Moscow and in France. But, for the past seven years, I have worked in a tiny hospital, a thousand miles from civilisation. And sometimes it seems like it's two hundred years from the latest developments in medicine. I think that we provide a good service; I'm proud of what our staff manages. But sometimes…' He smiled and went on. 'I have to remember that nursing skill is as important as drugs and machines.'

He looked over her shoulder. 'The postnatal ward is just there. Could we perhaps see Katya, the lady whose baby you delivered yesterday?'

She realised he was deliberately changing the subject. Well, she could sympathise. 'I'm sure we could. Wait here and I'll just ask the Sister if it's all right.'

'You do not have the right to walk straight in?'

'Well, we could walk straight in but we won't. It's polite to ask.'

He nodded thoughtfully. 'Sisters are as protective of their wards in England as they are in Russia?'

'A Sister's ward is her kingdom. She will fight to defend it against unwelcome intruders.'

'I know the feeling,' he said.

When Carly went to see her, Sister Maureen Kelly was very willing to let Alex in her ward. Carly realised that the hospital bush telegraph had been at work—word had spread about the new Russian doctor. And, when they met, Alex charmed the woman although he hardly said a word. 'Call me Maureen,' she told him warmly.

It shouldn't have surprised Carly but it did. She knew she had been affected by the appearance of Alex. Why shouldn't other women feel the same? But the idea that she was in some sort of competition for Alex's attention irritated her considerably. Not that she was interested in him, she told herself. Not in that way.

Maureen even accompanied the two of them down the ward, came into the little side ward with them. 'If there's anything she needs, you can translate for us,' she said.

Alex looked at her in surprise. 'I thought her husband had been to see her—that he spoke good English, that he had spoken to you at some length.'

'He has been in and he's coming in later this morning,' Maureen said amiably. 'But something might have come up.'

In the event there was little translation to be done. All the conversation went on in swift liquid Russian. Carly could follow much of what was being said, just by the actions. Alex asked how Katya was and was told she was much better, if a little sore. He looked at the baby, smiled and turned to congratulate the mother. There was a question and she answered…Olga. Alex looked at the baby again and said something about Olgushka. Obviously a childish form of the name. Then Alex and Katya looked at Maureen and Carly, and Alex said, 'Once again, Katya wishes to thank you both for what you have done. She will be eternally grateful to you all.'

Smiling and nodding, they left Katya to rest. And as they walked up the ward Maureen said, 'If you've got a minute, Carly, would you mind having a look at baby Noah? I'm a bit worried about him. The SHO was in earlier; she's rushed off her feet, poor girl. She said she'd come back and have another look, but if you could take a look now…'

'What's the problem?'

'It's just that baby Noah's oxygen requirements have increased slightly. He's not tolerating all of his feeds and he seems to be a bit out of sorts in general.'

'Happy to have a quick look,' Carly said. And then she wondered. Alex was here as a doctor—

but all she had seen him do so far was wipe the sweat from the brow of a woman in labour. Just how good a doctor was he? 'Would you like to look at this baby, Alex?' she asked.

'I'd be happy to.'

And Mrs Forsythe was happy too for him to examine her baby.

Maureen had work to do. Reluctantly, she left them to it and sent down a junior nurse to assist. Carly watched as Alex checked the baby's notes, gently undressed him, warmed his stethoscope before placing it on the baby's chest. His hands were gentle but assured; he knew exactly what he was doing. And finally he said, 'Baby Noah here has got an infection. I want a lumbar puncture, a full septic infection screen. He's to be transferred to the neo-natal unit. I want a cannula put in and some antibiotics.' He turned to the nurse. 'Would you fetch…?'

'Alex,' Carly said gently, 'could we have a word for a moment?'

He looked at her in surprise. 'You disagree with my diagnosis? Carly, this is…'

'A word for a moment?'

He followed her outside the little ward. His face had taken on that shut-down look that she had seen before. He might have feelings—but no way was he going to show them to the world.

'Carly, I assure you that this is definitely an infection that needs…'

'I know it is. I agree with you entirely. But we just looked at baby Noah as a favour to Maureen. You're not the baby's doctor; neither at the moment am I. What we do is report our suggestions to Maureen and she'll ensure that those suggestions are acted on. By the proper doctor.'

'This is wasting time! That baby needs treatment.'

'It is not wasting time! It is acting in a proper, a professional manner and that baby will be treated by his own doctor just as quickly as if you did it. Alex, you're supposed to be following me round today, just observing and seeing how we do things here.'

He said nothing for a while. Then, 'I thought it was only Russia that was being strangled by red tape. Very well, if you are sure the baby will not suffer.'

I'm the one that's suffering here, Carly thought, having to explain what should be obvious to a man who's sure that he's always right. 'The baby will not suffer,' she repeated. 'Now, let's go and report to Maureen.'

Maureen, pleased that her suspicions had been right, phoned and arranged for the SHO to return at once. Alex said he'd like to have a word with the doctor when she returned and Carly felt that she could at least allow him this. Then they had to wait.

Maureen went to arrange things for the SHO's return, leaving Carly alone with Alex. Alex stood silent, an implacable figure in the corner of Maureen's office. The atmosphere was decidedly chilly but it was Alex who eventually broke the silence.

'You're right, of course,' he said. 'And I suppose that means that I was wrong.'

'Right?' Carly asked. 'Wrong? What are we talking about?'

He seemed uncomfortable and Carly realised that this confession was something of an effort for him. He didn't like being wrong—or having to admit it. Hesitantly, he started, 'This is a large teaching hospital; it has a vast variety of medical staff. In order to make best use of medical skills there must be protocols, a clear understanding of who does what. It's like an army—you have to have a chain of command, you can't have people deciding that they know best and acting without telling anyone else. But that's what I appear to do, isn't it, Carly?'

She thought of his appearance the day before in the Delivery Room. 'Perhaps there's some truth there,' she said uneasily. 'But I'm sure you're trying to do the best for the patient.'

'I am.' Said with absolute certainty—now that was the Alex that she recognised. He went on, 'I can only say that at my small hospital we tend to be short-staffed. At times my senior nurses will take decisions that should more properly be taken by doctors. If they see a problem—they try to deal with it. I have encouraged this.'

'Not an army but a band of guerrillas,' Carly said with a grin.

He smiled back. 'Guerilla warfare on disease. I like that.'

'Tell me more about your nurses. I…'

Alice Newman, the SHO, entered the room. 'Have I missed something?' she asked, obviously alarmed.

Carly sighed to herself; it was time to be formal again. She had wanted to find out more about Alex's background but…he was here to specialise in children with infectious diseases, and to teach other doctors about treatment. So she sat back to watch him work as a teacher.

She might have guessed; he was good. He didn't tell Alice what was wrong, merely suggested that there were things that she should consider, look into. Then he sent her to look at the patient again.

'Noah will now get the treatment he needs?' he asked Carly with a smile.

'He'll get it. And the SHO will have become a slightly better doctor. Isn't that a good result?'

'Couldn't be better,' Alex agreed.

Maureen re-entered the room. 'Now I've almost got a peaceful ward,' she said to Carly and Alex with a happy smile. 'Only one problem left. And that's a personal not a medical problem.'

Alex looked at her curiously. 'A personal problem? How is that?'

Maureen shrugged. 'We've got someone, Maria Squires, who's taking as much of our time as the rest of the ward put together. She's one of those patients—you know the ones who've read a book or two, who think they know everything. She doesn't agree with the medication we've given her and she's refusing to feed the baby when and how we tell her. She says a mother always knows best. And in this case she's wrong. All she wants is an argument.'

'She has treatment, in a ward like this! And she argues?'

Carly and Maureen both looked at Alex. Carly thought it was amazing—not a muscle on Alex's bleak face appeared to have changed, and yet it was obvious he was angry.

'There are always patients who think they know better, who have to argue,' Carly said. 'Surely you have that too?'

'We do have it. And we deal with it. Maureen, might I speak to this patient? Not to treat her, of course—just to talk?'

Maureen shrugged. 'I can't see it doing any harm. We haven't been able to do much with her. But I really must finish these papers; I can't come down with you. She's in the last bed on the left.'

'Carly and I will go together,' Alex said and, before Carly knew what was happening, he had taken her arm and was easing her out of the Sister's room.

'I'm not sure about this,' Carly said uneasily. 'Handling this woman might take a bit of delicacy. And you do seem to tackle problems a bit bull-headed.'

'Some problems are universal. I have women in my wards whose great-grandfathers played polo with human heads. And yet underneath they are no different from this Maria Squires.'

'They aren't?' Carly asked faintly.

'No, they are not. Carly, please, let me deal with this woman my way. Afterwards you can complain if you wish.'

Carly winced. Looking after Alex was more difficult than she had anticipated. But, 'All right,' she said.

They found Mrs Squires, a thin-faced woman who stared at them as they approached. Carly realised that she had been dismissed after the first glance. But Alex earned a much longer gaze.

'Who are you?' Maria Squires said sharply.

Carly, remembering what she had just promised, said nothing. Equally silent, Alex drew the curtains round the bed. Then he stood looking down at the patient, his face bleak and forbidding.

'You're not the doctors I saw before,' Mrs Squires said after a while.

Alex remained silent, standing unmoving by the side of the bed. He was a big man and, for some reason, standing perfectly still seemed to make him seem bigger. His body might have been carved out of stone, Carly thought. She looked at his sombre face—that too might have been stone. There was no anger showing—nothing so human.

'Aren't you going to say anything?' This time there was a definite waver in Mrs Squires's voice.

Still no answer. The silence stretched out. Then, finally, in his deep voice, Alex said, 'Why are you refusing our professional help, Mrs Squires? Do you want your baby to be ill?'

What little colour was left in Maria Squires's face promptly disappeared. 'You can't talk to me like that,' she choked.

'I can. I am a doctor. And your actions are jeopardising the well-being of your child. Do you understand that?'

'I'm only doing what I think best for my…'

'Your best is wrong, Mrs Squires.'

He stared at the now-silent woman for a minute longer and then moved round to the other side of the bed to where her baby slept in his cot. He put a finger to the side of the baby's face, stroked it a moment. His own face was hidden from Maria Squires, but Carly could see it and was amazed at the transformation. There was so much caring!

But, when he turned back to the mother, the previous bleak expression had returned. 'You understand that the treatment you have here has been worked out over many years. It is the best there is. The advice you are given by doctors and nurses has been tried and proved. That too is the best. In the interests of your baby, you should remember that, Mrs Squires. Right?'

'Right,' Maria Squires quavered.

'Good.' Alex picked up the notes at the bottom of the bed. 'I see you did not take your medication this morning. I will send down a nurse and you will take it now. Is that understood?'

'Yes, Doctor.'

'Good.'

He was turning to leave when she asked, 'Will you be seeing me again, Doctor?'

'I'll take an interest in your progress,' Alex answered. 'And in the progress of your child.

Good morning, Mrs Squires.' He smiled at the stunned woman, nodded at Carly to follow him and they walked back down the ward.

Carly was seething. 'I agreed not to say anything,' she said when they were out of earshot, 'but it was hard. Do you always treat patients like that? Alex, you bullied her!'

'I did not bully her. I did not raise my voice and I was perfectly polite.'

'Some people can shout quietly, and you're one. It's frightening. That woman only gave birth a couple of days ago and…'

'And because of her stupidity she was threatening the health of her child. She was also making hard-working staff have to work even harder. It was necessary that someone told her. And I did.'

Carly sighed. 'There are some things we just can't agree on,' she said. 'But I suspect you've improved matters even if I don't agree with your methods. Now, it's mid-morning. Shall we have a quick break?'

'All doctors run on caffeine,' he told her.

* * *

The doctors' room was unusually quiet; there were only the two of them there. He offered to make her more of his black tea, but now she said she preferred coffee. She felt she'd had quite sufficient of his Russian civilisation for a while. But she was still fascinated by Alex.

'You had a face as black as thunder when you talked to Mrs Squires,' she said as they sat with their drinks. 'But your expression changed when you looked down at her baby. You love babies, don't you?'

It was a while before he replied. Then he said, 'Yes, I do.'

'But you have no children of your own?'

'No.' A curt monosyllable. The subject was obviously closed.

But Carly still wanted to know more about him. Surely it wasn't too impolite to ask? 'You're not married, then?'

Then she blinked. Why had she not asked this question before? She realised that she had taken it for granted that Alex wasn't married. Why should she do that? And now she had asked the question, why was his answer so important to her?

She didn't know how he did it. His face seemed not to change—but she could divine at once what he was feeling. Now his expression was cold, she winced when she saw it.

'I was married. My wife died some years ago.'

'And you never…?'

'One wife is enough for any man.'

Carly realised that this was the first time she had seen any suggestion of true, personal feeling. She had seen his love for children but this time his feelings were for himself. 'I'm sorry,' she said, 'I didn't mean to upset you. Did she…?'

'I am not upset. She is dead and I have accepted that. There is no point in going back over what cannot be altered.'

Carly shivered at the chill in his voice. She had been warned off; he didn't want to talk. But she wanted to hear! She wanted to know so much more about him. How could she change his mood?

'I've finished my coffee,' she said, 'and I'm

still in need of more caffeine. Could I change my mind and have some of your tea?'

His face lightened a little. 'Of course. In time I will convert you to my style of drinking.'

And when he returned with her tea his face was different again—now more thoughtful. She had seen this expression before; it was when he had thought about something but was keeping the conclusion to himself. She had wondered if she might probe a little more about his wife, but before she could ask he said, 'Are you married, Carly?'

The use of her name felt strangely intimate, as if inviting confidences. And she was taken back a little; she was supposed to be questioning him, not the other way round. Still, he had asked. 'No, I'm not married. I want to get my training over first.'

'Get your training over and get married,' he said softly.

He took her hand, turned it over as if to examine it. This was the first time he had touched her—as a person that was, not a colleague. And she felt a shiver of excitement. Her hand looked small in his, but he was so gentle.

'There is no engagement ring,' he said. 'You have no man in waiting? Surely someone as attractive as you must be at least engaged?'

It was hard answering him; she was quite happy to sit there in silence. But eventually she managed to gasp, 'There is no man in waiting, I'm quite fancy free. As I said, I want to get my training over first.'

'You can always change your mind,' he said. He seemed reluctant to release her hand and for the moment she was quite happy to let him hold it. He went on, 'It's possible that in time you might…'

Behind them they heard the door start to open. Gently, he put her hand down and they both turned to see John Bennett enter. Carly felt half relieved at being interrupted. She was happy to question Alex but wasn't so sure that she wanted her own feelings examined.

'Morning!' John moved straight to the coffee table, poured himself a mug. 'Alex, how are you getting on with Carly here?'

'I'm enjoying myself and I am learning. John, I'm envious of your set-up here. The equipment, the buildings…' He shook his head. 'It's all too much.'

'Equipment and buildings is only half the story. What counts is staff. You know that. Now, Carly, thanks for looking after Alex this morning, but now I'm going to let you get on with your work uninterrupted. Alex, you come with me and we'll talk about your programme.'

'Of course,' said Alex. He turned to Carly and said formally, 'Thank you for your instructions this morning, Dr Sinclair. I feel I have learned with you. Perhaps we will meet later in the day.'

'I hope so,' she replied. 'I've enjoyed being with you, Dr Braikovitch.' She wished John hadn't arrived when he had; she wanted to go on talking to Alex. Perhaps later.

But they didn't meet again. Carly's duties took her all over the Delivery Suite and she expected to see him in some ward or delivery room. But no sign of him or John.

By late afternoon she had to admit it to herself. She wanted to see him again. Just out of curiosity, of course. There was nothing…there could be nothing… That episode in the Delivery Room had just been an accident, an odd blip in her uneventful life.

By the time she finally left work she was irritated because she hadn't seen him and angry with herself because she was irritated. Her afternoon hadn't been half so enjoyable as her morning.

CHAPTER THREE

CARLY couldn't settle. Usually she was perfectly happy in her flat, her home. The night before she had been happy, even though she had spent so much time thinking about Alex. But she had thought she had come to some sort of a conclusion—Alex couldn't be for her. Today she had spent the morning with him and he had turned out to be a more difficult and a more interesting person than she had realised. And a more attractive one. So tonight her flat offered little comfort. She had a problem—she didn't know what to do about Alex. And there was, of course, another side to the problem. What did Alex want? She just didn't know.

After her bath and her evening meal she tried to occupy herself. She opened her books but found she couldn't study. She tried to clean the flat; it was spotless already. How about ironing? All that needed doing was done. She turned on the television and all there was on was rubbish.

So she phoned her older brother, Jack. First there was the usual family gossip, the progress of the children to catch up on. Then the true purpose of the call. In an attempt at a casual voice, she asked, 'What do you know about this new Russian doctor—Dr Braikovitch? I've been showing him around this morning; he seems quite an interesting character.'

Jack laughed. 'He's more than interesting, he's incredible. John Bennett introduced us this afternoon; we had quite a long chat. Did you know that he's mastered two specialities? He's both a Paediatrics and an Obs and Gynae man. And, what's more, he's done more than his fair share of neonatal and paediatric surgery. Just to think of it makes my head whirl.'

'He seems a bit self-opinionated,' Carly ventured.

'He's entitled to be. As well as Russian, he

speaks perfect French and English. Taught himself English at first because that was the language of most medical research. He could have got to the top, been an internationally known doctor. Instead he opted to go back to the place where he was born. When the Soviet Union broke up in 1991, more than a few places were worse off than before. His home town was one of them. So now apparently he spends all his time running the hospital and raging against corruption and inefficiency.'

'He might be good but he certainly knows it,' Carly said.

Jack laughed. 'He's spent too much of his time among fools and rogues to accept them regularly. You know that while he's here he's being paid for and sponsored by a charity called MedAsia? In fact...' there was the rustle of papers '...as part of his contract he's going to give a talk about his work in Manchester this coming Saturday. There's going to be a collection of the great and the good to hear him. Lots of high-ranking medical people, and just as many high-ranking politicians. The press will be there in force and probably television as well.' Casually, Jack went on, 'I've got a ticket; I could get another if you'd like to come as well?'

Striving to be equally casual, Carly said, 'It might be interesting and I'm doing nothing that night. Yes, get me a ticket if you can.'

There were a few more minutes of general chat and then they rang off.

She felt a little calmer after the phone call, though it was hard to know why. Perhaps because she had made a decision. Just a decision to find out more about Alex.

Why was she so interested in someone she had only just met? She was the cautious, the careful one. She was wary of men; she had been caught and hurt by one before and had sworn it would never happen again. If she did ever fall for a man—which was unlikely—it would be after a long period of acquaintance, a long slow getting to know each other. She didn't think much of the idea of love being like a lightning strike. Though yesterday something like lightning had struck her.

No matter. She would be safe enough in the company of her brother Jack. Then she wondered. Safe from what?

There was a call from John early the next morning. 'Carly, I'm imposing on you but I hope you don't mind. Will you take Alex round with you for the rest of this week? Probably just the mornings. I think it's the easiest way of showing him the way we do things, our protocols and so on. It'll take the place of our regular induction programme.'

'Sounds like a good plan.' Carly kept her voice casual even though she could feel her pulse beating harder than usual. 'Is Alex happy with the idea?'

'He should be; he suggested it. Said he learned a lot about the hospital from you yesterday.'

'I think I learned from him. It's just that our ways of doing things are sometimes different from his style.'

John laughed. 'Alex seems more interested in results than the means used to get them. I know our way is better really, but sometimes…

Anyway, Carly, I gather you're working in the Antenatal ward this morning. I'll send him along to meet you there.'

'I'll be waiting.' She rang off.

So Alex had specifically asked that she could show him round, had said that he had learned from her. She wasn't exactly aware of teaching him anything yesterday. If anything the opposite had happened—she'd learned from him.

Perhaps he just wanted her company? She wasn't quite sure what she felt about this. When she thought about it, being with Alex yesterday had been almost completely professional. Apart from that short conversation in which he had told her his wife was dead, had asked her if she had any plans to marry. And she'd been half glad, half sorry when John had interrupted them. She had ventured on to Alex's personal territory—and then he had done the same to her. It had been unsettling. But she knew it was a conversation that wasn't yet over. Whatever, she'd better get down to Antenatal.

He was already in the ward when she got there,

sitting in the Sister's office. As Carly entered, the Sister, a newly promoted nurse called Amy Marsh, looked up, a slight expression of disappointment on her face. For a man who didn't say too much, Alex seemed to charm an awful lot of women, Carly thought, a little sourly. And then he smiled at Carly, and she knew how he did it.

He nodded at Carly, turned back to Amy and then Carly had to revise her opinion. He wasn't charming Amy—he was teaching her. Continuing their conversation, Amy asked, 'So tell me, when should you suspect spinal meningitis? I've never even seen a case.'

'In the past seven years I've only dealt with two myself,' Alex said. 'Happily, it's very rare. First of all, the baby is obviously very ill. There is evidence of sepsis and you might find a stiff neck, an inturning eye or bulging fontanelles. In these cases, if a consultant isn't in charge already, you send for one at once. Massive antibiotics is the only possible cure, and even they are often unsuccessful. Meningitis is a nightmare.'

'Any risk of infection? I mean across the ward.'

Alex shook his head. 'No extra-special pre-cautions. Just the normal standards of cleanli-ness.'

'Right,' said Amy. And Carly saw that she had been taking notes. Once again, a slightly sour thought crossed her mind. Was the pretty Sister interested in learning or interested in Alex?

Perhaps fortunately then, Alice Newman, the SHO, put her head round the door. 'Carly, I'm glad you're here. There's a bit of a problem and…oh! Good to see you again, Dr Braikovitch.'

'What's the problem, Alice?' Carly asked, feeling a little tired of having to cope with the re-actions of the female staff when they met Alex, then feeling annoyed with herself for caring.

'Mrs Arden. She brought herself in, thirty weeks pregnant, very worried because she thinks she's been bleeding. But I've examined her; I think the blood is in her urine.'

Alex looked at Carly, raised his eyebrows. Carly nodded. He hadn't quite started yet, but

Alex was to have the rank of senior Registrar. He was to be her superior; it was his job to answer questions like this. But it was good of him to request her permission.

'Colour of the blood?' Alex asked Alice.

'Frank red. Oh, and her haemoglobin's down.'

'And she's more than worried. She feels generally low.'

'That's right.'

Alex nodded judiciously. 'So your first impression is? Tell us; it doesn't matter if you're wrong.'

Alice hesitated. 'Well, I don't like involving another firm if it's not necessary. But I suspect it's not our problem. Haematuria like this usually isn't an obstetrics matter; I think the patient needs a urologist's or a nephrologist's care. But they'll need an obs and gynae person hanging round just in case.'

'Well done,' Alex said. 'I agree entirely. Carly?'

'I agree too. I'll get in touch with the other people, Alice. We'll have them down here as soon as we can. And I'd like you to be standing by when they come. Any problem that seems to be ours—get in touch with me.'

Carly reached for the phone—and her bleeper sounded. It was going to be one of those days.

She checked the number, rang back. 'Possible problem in Delivery Room number three,' she said to Alex. 'We're not needed yet, but the midwife would like someone to have a look in ten minutes or so. I'll just phone Urology and then I'll show you where you get scrubs from.'

'I like to keep busy,' he said.

They changed into scrubs and on their way towards the Delivery Room, Carly said, 'I heard you're giving a talk in Manchester on Saturday.'

'I am. I'm afraid I'll largely be talking about controlling diseases in distant—almost primitive—parts of the world, but—would you like to come?'

'I would. I've already asked my brother to get me a ticket.'

'I see. Why this sudden interest in diseases in central Asia?'

She decided to be honest, to shock him if need be. 'I will be interested in infections in other parts of the world, even if I never go there. But I'm more interested in listening to you. I want to know just what kind of person you are.'

He took her arm, stopped her walking further. His face was serious as he looked down at her. 'Why should you be interested in the kind of person I am? I'm just a colleague; we work together. In three months we will part and probably never see each other again.'

This was not the cautious, careful woman that she thought she was. She said, 'In the Delivery Room where we first met. Something happened there, I don't know what. But you felt it too, didn't you?'

His grip on her arm tightened. He scowled at her and said, 'It was just a meeting of two people who had a problem that they had to deal with together and...'

'Alex! I know one certain thing about you

already. You won't lie; you just can't be bothered to go to the trouble. So don't try to lie to me now. You did feel something, didn't you?'

The silence between them stretched and stretched. Then, 'Yes, I felt it,' he growled.

'Then we start from there.'

'We start? And where do you think we will go?'

She shook her head in bewilderment. 'I just don't know.'

It wasn't a serious problem in Delivery Room number three. But it was a problem that made Carly feel glad that the birth was not taking place at home.

She introduced Alex to the midwife and Alex courteously asked if it was all right if he could stay. When given permission he went straight to the patient's head, introduced himself and took a cloth to dab at the heated face. Just as he had with Katya, Carly remembered. It was obvious that, for Alex, people came before the strict practice of medicine. Only after a couple of minutes did he turn to hear what the midwife had to say.

'Mrs Brant has been pushing for nearly an hour now,' the midwife explained. 'The baby is in the occipito-posterior position and mother is nearly exhausted. The baby's heart rate is starting to drop and it's slow to return to the base line. I think we need a bit of help to get the baby out.'

For the first time, Alex didn't offer an opinion at once. So Carly asked him, 'What do you think, Dr Braikovitch? Ventouse or forceps extraction?'

'I prefer ventouse myself. But what is your opinion?'

'I think ventouse too. Would you like to do it?'

'I'd be happy to.'

It struck her that he was happier working than talking about it. And she had to admire his skill. The suction cup was fitted swiftly to the baby's head, gentle traction applied. His hands were deft, his knowledge complete. He managed to talk to the mother, to reassure her. And, more quickly than Carly would have thought possible, the baby was delivered. Alex inspected the baby's head for the chignon—the area of bruising and oedema where the cup had fitted. All was well. It had been a good birth.

'I got the impression that you were happier working on your own,' Carly said as they walked down the corridor afterwards. 'You could have made more use of the midwife; she's very competent.'

He shrugged. 'I get used to working on my own. Help is good if it's there. For me it often isn't—so I have to manage somehow.'

Once again she wondered about this complex man. Had he always been self-assured to the point of arrogance? Or had he had to learn to be that way?

'You've finished with me now,' she told him when they had changed out of their scrubs. 'You're in Theatre this afternoon. John said that you're going to watch Jack correct an oesophageal atresia. In fact you might be doing a bit of the work yourself. And I've got permission to come in and watch too. But it's an hour before we're needed, so shall we go and have lunch together?'

'Lunch? You mean stop for a meal in the middle of the day? Dr Sinclair, you'll get me into bad habits. For lunch I usually have a mug of tea by my desk side. But yes, today I would like lunch. Where?'

She could tell he was joking by the smile on his face. 'There's quite a good canteen,' she told him.

They walked into the canteen together, queued for their meal and then found a table just for the two of them. Carly couldn't see any of her particular friends so they sat alone. And after a moment she realised this perhaps wasn't such a good idea. Her brother Toby came in, smiled and waved at her but didn't come over to sit with them. Other people she vaguely knew came and passed her by. And when they sat down Carly could see heads getting together.

'You look a little disturbed,' Alex said. 'You're looking round as if to find someone.'

She decided to be honest with him. 'I didn't think this through. We're sitting together. Just the two of us. In this hospital that means we're an item. In fact it's practically a statement that we're about to get engaged. I'm sure my friends are deliberately leaving us alone together.'

'So I am compromising you. The sweet Dr Sinclair—the Good of the Good, the Bad and the Ugly.'

She blushed when she heard this. 'Someone's told you that silly story, have they? It's not fair because it's not true. It's a joke. Jack's not ugly, Toby's not bad and I'm not...' She realised she had left herself in trouble.

He smiled. 'In your case I think the saying is true. You are good.' He gathered his plate, knife and fork. 'I must not embarrass you. I shall leave the table and you can beckon to the next of your friends who enters.'

'Don't you dare move!' She put out a hand to stop him. 'I want you to stay.'

'And risk the gossip?'

'Gossip is gossip. Who cares, anyway?' She said it bravely and tried to persuade herself that she meant it. But in fact she was entirely uncertain as to what she wanted.

Changing the subject might help. Swallowing

a mouthful of salad, she asked, 'You've only just arrived really, but do you expect to enjoy working here?'

'Very much so. I like the building, I like the equipment.' He stared at her. 'I very much like the staff.'

Carly decided to let this remark pass. 'I would have thought that there's not an awful lot new. Medicine is medicine.'

'Perhaps so. What I do miss in my own hospital—one thing I miss—is company. I am largely on my own. There are just two other doctors to consult; they are husband and wife and we are all worked off our feet. There are no new ideas, no new techniques, little conversation. Here it is better.'

'How do you manage with so few doctors?'

He smiled. 'It is a problem and I suspect that my solution would not please many doctors. If I can't teach young doctors, then I can teach experienced nurses. And I do teach them. Then I give my senior nurses far more responsibility than would normally be considered proper. They diagnose, take decisions, perform minor surgery, prescribe drugs.'

'In effect, you promote nurses to be doctors?'

'Let's just say that I'd rather be in the care of one of my experienced nurses than in the care of a newly qualified doctor.'

'You're a risk-taker,' she told him. 'Very unusual in a doctor. I think I like it.'

'It works well for both staff and patients.'

She had to ask. 'So have you ever thought of moving? I gather you've had other job offers and you have done your time there.'

He shrugged, then looked down at his plate. He tried to make his voice casual but she thought that for once he didn't quite succeed. 'The place needs a hospital and a senior doctor. If not me, then who? The work has to be done by someone.'

'That's what matters most,' she said. She felt he was not telling her the entire truth—he wasn't lying but he was concealing something. Still, for the moment she'd let it pass. Just for the moment. 'What else do you miss?'

There was a long pause and once again she

wondered if he was going to answer. At first she had thought this waiting before replying was bad manners on his part. Now she was beginning to suspect it was something else. It was the action of a man who had a vast amount of responsibility and no one to share it with. The loneliness of command. Words had to be thought about, weighed for meaning.

Eventually he said, 'You're going to hear me talk on Saturday. Wait until then. I'll answer your questions after that if you wish.' He glanced at his watch. 'Time we were going?'

Well, no, it wasn't; they had a good ten minutes before they needed to move. But Carly felt that he needed to escape. 'I'll take you where we go to scrub up,' she said.

Alex sat in a cubicle in the changing room and thought. He was in doubt. This was unusual for him. Usually he knew what needed to be done and went ahead to do it. No matter how difficult. If decisions had to be made—then he'd made them quickly.

He had to think about Carly. He…he liked her a lot. At the moment, accepting that was as far as he was prepared to go. Though there would have to be more. From the first time he had seen her in the Delivery Room, he had been aware that there was something between them, some bond had been tied that would be near impossible to untie.

He was a doctor. He understood life and death; he did not readily believe in superstitions, in folk lore. But he was also Russian. He knew that there were some things that were not easily explicable by science and logic. Even in England he would never shake hands with someone across the threshold of their home. He had to step inside. He knew—of course he knew—that he would not be disturbing the house spirit, bringing bad luck. That was a foolish Russian superstition. But he still would not do it.

So what about Carly? He knew what he felt for her. He suspected—no, he knew—that she felt the same about him. And this was not something that might lead to a short affair, to be forgotten as soon as he moved back home. This was something deeper, stronger than that.

So what was he to do?

One thing was certain. He could not take her back with him. The life was too hard, the conditions too severe for her. His home was not the place for a tenderly nurtured British girl. All right, he guessed she was tough. But life out there was even tougher. He owed it to her to discourage her. They had known each other only for such a short time and yet already he could sense something growing between them. It had to stop.

That would be hard on himself. Just for a while he had glimpsed the possibility of a different kind of life, one in which he could share his thoughts, his feelings. And it seemed so appealing. Then he thought of his life so far. Once he had had that kind of relationship. And, when it ended so cruelly, he had vowed never to risk himself again. Yes, whatever was between Carly and himself had to stop.

He pulled on his scrubs, went to scrub up. Then he walked into Theatre, looked round him. There was Carly. He gave her a brief nod. A moment's envy as he saw the equipment, the skilled staff standing by, even the lighting. On one evil winter's night some years ago even the emergency lights had failed in his hospital and he had had to finish an operation by oil light. A small smile spread across his face as he remembered. The operation had been a success. The child had lived.

Alex held out his hands for the nurse to ease gloves on to them, adjusted his mask. The patient was wheeled in, already anaesthetised. Jack followed. He beckoned Alex to come over, to stand by his side To the Theatre at large, Jack said, 'This is a case of oesophageal atresia. The oesophagus is in two sections, instead of being one complete tube. We will join the two sections.' Then he stretched out his hand. The scrub nurse put a scalpel into it. Jack made the first cut.

'Is this any different from what you would do, Alex?' Jack asked as he entered the chest between the fourth and fifth rib.

Alex shook his head. 'Your technique is almost

identical to mine. But it's always good to watch another professional at work. Apart from anything else, it tells you that you've been getting it right all those times in the past.'

There was laughter at this. Alex watched as Jack performed the most difficult part of the operation, the anastomosis, or joining of the two sections. The join had to be strong and leak-proof. He did it well. Then he turned to Alex and said, 'Would you like to close, Alex?'

This was the easy part. But Alex knew he was still an unknown quantity to most of the people in the room and he felt the little shiver of interest pass through those watching. Just how good was this newcomer? This was a test.

'I would indeed,' he said, and stretched out his hand to the scrub nurse.

A simple closure. Pulling together the vessels, muscles, flesh that had been slit, sewing them as neatly as possible, making sure that they were— not waterproof but blood proof.

He worked as he always did, at his own speed. And somewhere in the back of his mind he heard the gasps of surprise, even felt the uneasy movement of Jack by his side. But he would not be put off; he had to concentrate. And when he had finished, suturing the long opening cut from the right side of the chest to under the tip of the shoulder blade, there was a mutter of appreciation from those gathered round, even a small round of applause.

'Great job,' said Jack, nodding his approval. 'Let's have a breather before the next one.'

A little crowd of staff gathered round him in the corridor outside—Carly was one of them, Alex noticed.

'I've never seen suturing done so quickly,' Jack said. 'But you did a brilliant job. Where did you learn to move like that?'

Alex shrugged. 'I find I have to do a lot of suturing, often of accidents rather than operations. And as mine is the only hospital for a hundred miles, many patients arrive very late. We do what we can, but I have had children die on the table who would have been saved if we had seen them earlier.'

A silence, then, 'That must be very hard,' someone said.

'It is. But we live with it. Here in A and E you have the Golden Hour, don't you—get a seriously injured person within an hour of their accident and there is a good chance of their surviving. Well, if we're lucky, we have a Golden Day. Then, once they're on the operation table, a Golden Five Minutes.'

He could hear the sighs of sympathy in the little crowd. Well, he was here to tell people about conditions, he might as well do the job properly. 'And I have no proper anaesthetist. I have a nurse—I sent her to Moscow on a six-month intensive training course. Together we make quite a good team.'

'A six-month training course!' It was Jack's horrified anaesthetist speaking. 'I had to do medicine for six years before I even started on anaesthetics! And then there was another five years.'

'Better a six-month course than nothing at all,' Alex said simply.

'Time we all were moving,' Jack said. 'Alex,

once again, that was a brilliant piece of work. But I'm not going to encourage my students to work at your pace. I couldn't match it myself. Are you coming back in with us?'

Alex shook his head. 'Thank you for letting me observe,' he said. 'And I hope to do so again. But now I have an appointment with John Bennett and he…'

'And he's here.' John smiled as he joined them. 'Carly, could you please come as well? We're in my office.'

The little group dispersed. Time to get back to work.

As well as concentrating on infant and childhood disease, with special responsibility for infectious diseases, Alex was also to get involved with cases of maternal malnutrition, and John was eager for him to begin.

'You'll often deal with the cases we get referred to us by Social Services—pregnant women or mothers with newborn babies who don't seem to be able to properly feed either themselves or their children,' he said. 'We're getting more and more of these women; there wasn't a quarter of the number when I started training. But now it's a growing problem.'

'It is something I can deal with,' Alex said. 'I have had much experience of it.'

'Which is why we'd like to benefit from your expertise in this area,' agreed John. He handed Alex a bunch of keys. 'We've organised an office and small treatment room for you, next to the Delivery Suite. It's handy for both the Obs and Gynae work, and for the cases we get sent to us from A and E. Secretarial assistance—you'll have to share a secretary with two other senior Registrars, but I'm sure there'll be no problem there.'

'And the specific timetable?' Alex asked.

John handed him a folder. 'As you see, you'll have a set of clinics and ward rounds of your own. But it's going to take some arranging to have responsibilities transferred, so I suspect you'll spend much of your time over the next fortnight picking up patients in A and E, admitting them and then seeing to their care. You'll get a lot of referrals from GPs. Occasionally you'll make home visits. And I've timetabled you to give a series of lectures, to medical students and junior staff, on infectious diseases and their handling.'

Carly felt herself flinch. Did Alex know just how busy he was going to be?

But Alex didn't seem to mind. He was leafing through the folder John had given him, obviously approving of its contents. 'I'm ready to start work,' he said. 'This is good.'

'One more thing,' John said, and there was something in his voice that made Carly suddenly alert. 'Alex, you're a brilliant clinician but you're a stranger, both in this hospital and in the city. There'll be mistakes you might make, procedures you might not know about. So I think you should work together with someone who knows their way around. I was thinking of Carly sharing your office for the next three months and acting as your junior.'

Carly's mouth dropped open; she felt bewildered. This was the last thing she had expected.

And she didn't know what she felt about it. On one level, working with or for Alex would be a wonderful chance for her to learn. Professionally, she knew it was a great offer. But personally? She had enjoyed being with him over the past few days. But there had always been that…fear or apprehension…of what he might come to mean to her. She had steeled herself to work closely with him, thinking that quite shortly she'd see much less of him. But now? Being thrown together like this?

She became aware that the three of them were silent. She looked from face to face. Alex, as ever, gave nothing away. His expression was completely blank. John just looked thoughtful.

And it was John who broke the silence. 'You'll both have to think about this,' he said, 'make up your own minds. I'm not going to force staff into arrangements that they're uncomfortable with. Discuss it between you, see what you think. And if either or both of you aren't happy then we'll sort out something else. I need to be off now, so if you could let me know some time today…' He stood up, nodded at them both and left.

Carly looked at Alex. 'What do you think, Alex?' she said.

His reply was quiet, formal. 'I have watched you work, listened to you talk. I think you would be the perfect choice to work with me. We will get on, then?'

'I'm sure we will. Will you tell John that the arrangement goes ahead as he planned? We'll meet and talk later, shall we, but for now there are things I have to deal with.'

She turned and walked away. They could have discussed what was happening between them now, she thought… No, they couldn't. Thoughts, emotions, worries, churned inside her. How was she going to cope with this? She just had to work out some way of being close to him and yet distant from him. It was going to be hard.

For a moment Alex stood motionless, watching her retreating form. Scrubs were an ugly, shape-less set of garments, but they could not hide her figure. In fact, perhaps they enhanced it. He allowed himself a minute to appreciate the line of leg, the trim waist and the graceful feminine sway to her body. Carly was beautiful. She was more than beautiful because she seemed unaware of it.

He was now thinking again about working with her. He wanted to and he knew she was hard-working and experienced; they would make a good team.

So they would make a good team. But not an hour ago he had decided that he was bad for her. He had decided to distance himself from her. And now they were to work together. He, iron-willed Alex, had failed at his first test.

Of course, now he had agreed this with her, he couldn't just ask for a change. It would be ill-mannered. So they'd have to stay together.

As he thought this, tried to persuade himself that this was the reason for keeping her, he knew he was deceiving himself. He was keeping her because he couldn't keep away.

* * *

Alex was travelling to Manchester with John and a group of dignitaries from the charity MedAsia. Carly was to go with Jack. This was to be a formal affair; she would have to dress accordingly. 'Not evening dress,' Jack had told her. 'But not jeans either.'

And she wanted to look smart; she wanted to make a small effort of her own. She took out the suit she had bought for her last big interview and not worn since. Black, with waisted short jacket, pencil skirt. A white silk shirt with a pendant that had been her mother's. A perfect example of the cool medical professional, she thought as she surveyed herself in the mirror.

She didn't ask herself why it was so important to look smart.

Jack raised his eyebrows when he picked her up. 'Making an effort, aren't we?' he said as he looked at her with obvious approval.

'You're looking pretty smart yourself,' she answered. 'I don't usually like these big formal get-togethers but I'm looking forward to this one.'

'Alex is quite a character, isn't he?' Jack said

neutrally and she wondered exactly what he meant.

The Practitioners' Hall was in the centre of Manchester and dated back to when the city had been a centre of world trade—and knew it. They were shown into a panelled hall, the walls lined with the gloomy pictures of self-satisfied Victorian dignitaries. They accepted a sherry each.

'Many more men than women here,' Carly muttered indignantly as they looked round.

'Many more women than there would have been when I started in medicine,' Jack told her. 'Look, I'm going for a word with an old pal over there. You okay on your own?'

'I'm fine,' she said. In fact she wanted to be on her own. It would give her chance to look round, to observe.

She could admit it to herself—she wanted to see Alex. And she soon spotted him in the centre of a group who were listening to him talk, apparently fascinated. Well, that was to be expected. She wasn't going to approach him;

she knew he was here on a mission. He had a point of view to get across.

The room was filled with well-dressed men, some with excellent figures. But Alex appeared to stand out. He was in the traditional man's formal outfit—like Jack, indeed like herself. Dark suit, gleaming white shirt, some sort of college tie. But he seemed to dominate the group he was with, be the automatic centre of attention. He was the most handsome—no, the most impressive—man there.

As she watched she saw an older man take him by the arm, say something to the group and then lead him away to another group. Obviously some dignitary was introducing him to as many people as was possible. Well, that was what he was here for.

He didn't seem to be smiling much. Not that he ever did. And this only made him more impressive. The brooding eyes, the high cheek bones, the mouth that could look so cruel—he seemed like a wolf in the middle of a herd of sheep. A wolf in sheep's clothing? Carly shivered.

There was a discreet announcement from a hidden microphone. The talk would start in five minutes; could members please take their seats? People started to drift towards the double doors at one end of the hall.

She saw him make excuses, break away from the group he was with. He looked round, saw her. And there was that thrill when their gazes locked.

He came over to her, smiled. 'Why didn't you come to say hello?' he asked. 'I was hoping you would. I looked for you, but I was talking and I…'

'You were busy,' she told him. 'Doing the job you are here for. It's important that you get on with these people. Important that you network.'

'Network?' He frowned, as if this was a new idea. 'I don't like it but I guess it has to be done.' Then he appeared to think of something more pleasant and he said, 'But I'll be glad to have someone friendly in the audience. Now I'm just going to dip my face in cold water ready to appear on stage.'

'You have lots of friends here,' she told him. 'Are you nervous?'

'No.' His voice was certain. 'It is easier to talk about things than do them. But I want what I say to be a success. It is important to people.'

She glanced round. The audience were now filing into the lecture theatre. They were largely unobserved. Not that it mattered. On impulse she reached up and kissed him.

She had intended to kiss him on the cheek. But somehow—perhaps he turned his head— she kissed him on the lips. It lasted longer than she had expected. And what was meant to be a simple salute between friends changed into something deeper and much more meaningful.

Shocked, she looked at him. 'That's for good luck,' she managed to croak. She gazed into those icy grey-blue eyes and saw something, just for a moment, that made her pulse race faster than it had done in years. He was not the ice-man that she had thought. He had feelings too, and could show them if he wanted.

A small smile. 'Good luck? I think I have it

already. I hope to see you afterwards.' And he was gone.

Carly turned to see Jack waiting to escort her into the lecture theatre.

CHAPTER FOUR

ALEX walked to the men's cloakroom. He was feeling bleak.

Carly had kissed him. Just for a moment it had been so good. It had transported him to a different life, one without responsibilities where he could do as he wished. And now he was feeling emotions, not new to him but repressed for many years. He had no time for love. This was not good!

And what was he doing to Carly? He had seen, had felt her response. He knew what she felt for him, knew also that in turn she had recognised his response. Even though he had tried to hide it.

He was a doctor. He knew that present pain was often necessary to prevent greater pain in the future. Somehow he would have to keep away from her. No, that would be too much. For him as well as for her. Somehow he would have to keep a distance between them—even though they were working together. It would hurt him as well as her. But he was used to pain.

Now he had a talk to give. He tore his mind away from personal problems. There was work to do.

'Giving a quick kiss to encourage the beleaguered man,' Jack joked as he took Carly's arm to escort her into the next room. 'And very good of you too.'

Still shaken by what had just happened, Carly mumbled a reply, trying to tell herself it had only been a kiss, nothing more. She'd just wanted to show her support, wish a colleague good luck. But this had been a signal. It had been the first…well, the first more intimate contact they'd had. And she knew that it had been waiting to happen since that first shattering exchange of glances in the Delivery Room.

Even Jack, her own brother, didn't notice

anything, she thought with a touch of desperation. This was something just between Alex and herself. What was she going to do?

They made their way into the lecture theatre. This was nothing like the hard-seated place where she had spent so many bottom-aching hours when she had been a student; this place had upholstered seats, comfortable arm rests, a pad and pen for each delegate.

She looked at the lecturer's desk below—the microphone, the glass of water for the speaker. All much as usual. Then the lights were dimmed, except over the desk, and two men entered to a scatter of polite applause.

One man was Alex, the other was the distinguished-looking man who Carly had seen ushering Alex from group to group. 'That's Sir Russell Crown,' Jack whispered. 'Used to be a doctor, now a member of the House of Lords and advisor to the government on all sorts of health matters. He's the President of MedAsia. Apparently Crown is his anglicised name. Family came from Russia in the nineteen-twenties.'

'Ladies and gentlemen, we are here to listen to Dr Alexander Braikovitch. He has had a full life—studying medicine in Moscow and then Paris. Since then his activities have been considerable...'

Carly blinked when she heard of the papers Alex had written, the work he had done.

'...and then he chose to move away from the cutting edge of medicine and take up residency in a small hospital in one of the loneliest and, dare I say it, most forgotten outlying regions of Russia. He is here to describe his work there. And to suggest how his experiences might some day affect us.'

More clapping as Sir Russell moved away from the microphone and Alex stepped forward.

'I didn't know Alex had done so much,' Carly whispered to Jack. 'It's amazing!'

'He could have gone right to the top, been an international medical star. He gave it all up to go to some God-forsaken bit of Northern Russia. It's a pity; it's a loss to medicine.'

'Not if that's what he wants.'

Alex stood behind the microphone, waited for

the paper rustling, the odd whisper to finish. He didn't speak at once. He just looked at his audience, unsmiling. Carly remembered it as a trick her old headmistress used to use. Only Alex was much better at it.

Eventually there was absolute silence in the room, a feeling of tension. It was almost a relief when he began to speak. It was only five minutes since Carly had heard that deep voice, with the slight foreign intonation that made it mysterious, seductive. But she still thrilled to it.

Surprisingly, his tone was almost conversational. He told them a little about working in one of the farthest regions of Russia, of working in an area that might in fact be Russia or possibly belong to one of the newly freed republics that were trying to establish themselves. Whatever, no one much cared for it. It was too far from anywhere to be worth arguing about. Communications were poor or non-existent. The nearest railway was three hundred miles away. There was a primitive landing strip for small planes but in winter the snow closed it down. So contact

with what might be called civilisation was difficult. Vital supplies took three days to arrive by
lorry. Often they didn't arrive at all.

His patients were drawn from a vast area and
were the descendants of nomads who had
roamed the steppes of central Asia.

'Some of these people live by subsistence
farming,' Alex said. 'But they are the descen-
dents of nomads and many of them are still wanderers. And this brings problems. Wanderers,
travellers, may bring new ideas, new goods to
trade. But they also bring diseases. The medical
history of the Western world is full of examples
of pandemics caused by the advent of travellers.
Think of the Black Death in fourteenth century
Britain. Or even something so apparently mild as
measles among the native Americans in the nineteenth century.'

Alex paused and went on, 'With cheap long-
distance flight, the world is becoming a smaller
place. Britain is becoming more cosmopolitan,
foreigners pass through here, settle here. And
some bring diseases. The problems that I have

to deal with at the moment—you may have to deal with in the next few years.'

Carly felt the uneasy movement of the audience. Alex's remark was unpleasant. But it was true.

'I deal with the usual diseases that might affect such an area as mine,' Alex went on. 'The diseases of poverty, of poor water supply, of inadequate diet, of ignorance. And the diseases that spread because of inadequate medical care. Among other conditions I have dealt with are brucellosis, hepatitis A and B, pneumonia, sepsis, tuberculosis, typhoid. Even an occasional case of malaria. Sadly, I have seen an increasing number of HIV cases. I want to devote the rest of my talk to considering the ways that these infections can be controlled, or even prevented. Not just in far off Central Asia. But possibly, some time soon, in diverse Britain.'

Carly realised that Alex now had his audience where he wanted them. They were held by his talk. When he finished the applause was deafening. A couple of people stood whilst still clapping; soon everyone stood and Alex was receiving a standing ovation. Carly stood and clapped too. She thought he deserved it.

There were questions after that—many questions. Alex handled them well, even a couple of times admitting that he had been asked a question to which he could think of no reasonable answer. Carly felt that the audience was taking to him even more. Medical men and politicians—people who by nature were cautious, suspicious even. But they liked and respected Alex.

Eventually Sir Russell felt he had to intervene. 'Ladies and gentlemen, I feel we have put our speaker through quite enough of an ordeal this evening so I will bring the meeting to a close. However, we will be taking a glass of wine now and there may be chance for some of you to speak to him later.'

More applause as Alex was escorted out of the lecture theatre. 'Sir Russell has set up a press conference,' Jack told her. 'Newspapers, magazines and at least one TV channel. Alex should get the publicity he needs.'

'Good,' Carly said. She was feeling—well, she was not sure what she was feeling. She had become accustomed to Alex as a medical colleague and a friend—perhaps something more than a friend. Now she was seeing him as something else—a public figure with an agenda that went beyond the personal. She had felt more comfortable with him before.

He had just made a very successful public speech. Probably he would get what he wanted out of it—publicity for his cause. But just before the speech she had kissed him, and she had felt that something had passed between them that was life-shaking.

Which was the more important to him—speech or kiss? She didn't know. She wasn't sure that she wanted to know. As so often, she felt vulnerable. She didn't know if this feeling was good for her.

Alex and Sir Russell now came back into the hall. The meeting with the journalists had taken place in a side room and was now over; Alex was free to meet more of the invited guests. Once again Sir Russell piloted Alex from group to group. No one was allowed to take up too much of his time, everyone was given the chance to speak to him personally. Carly realised just how effective Sir Russell was, what unobtrusive skills he was showing.

She hadn't quite realised it but she was staring at Alex. He was with a group; he looked up and for a moment their gazes clashed. He smiled at her and she blushed, even though she managed to smile back and then look away. There was something personal in his smile—a promise or an invitation, even? She was being silly!

Carly wrenched her attention from Alex and tried to concentrate on talking to Jack. They had interests in common, she thought. They were friends as well as being brother and sister— surely they could talk to each other? So she asked him about the history of the Practitioners' Hall and managed to be fascinated by some of the things that he told her. In fact it was interesting and when he explained about the…

'Carly and Jack. I'm so glad you are here.'

It was Alex! How had he managed to creep up on them without her noticing? She looked up at him, for the moment unable to speak. And where was Sir Russell?

Jack was shaking his hand. 'Super speech, Alex. You had the audience enthralled.'

'Glad you liked it. I found it a bit of a challenge. I'm not used to all this shaking hands and being nice to people.'

'You don't like being nice to people?' Carly asked, recovering.

'Not everyone. But I'm very impressed by Sir Russell. He's made everything easy for me.'

'Where is he?' Jack asked with a grin. 'He's been your chaperon all evening so far.'

'He needed to meet the press for a minute and I asked for a break. Said I wanted to talk to my friends, relax just for five minutes. And I came to you two.'

Us two? Carly thought. Jack and me? Then she looked into his eyes and guessed which friend he most wanted to talk to.

'There are still people Sir Russell wants me to

meet,' Alex went on, 'so he'll be back shortly and I gather I'm to be taken on to a smaller meeting. But I wish I could stay with you.'

'Being in demand is the price of fame,' Carly told him.

'And we'll have plenty of time together when we work,' Alex said. 'Now I must go.'

Carly looked after his retreating form and wondered.

It was only a short ride home to Liverpool. Jack and Carly were companionably silent, listening to soothing night-drive music on his radio. But after a while Jack asked, apparently casually, 'So how are you getting on with Alex, Carly? You seem to be seeing a lot of him and I gather you're going to work with him full-time.'

'I am going to work with him and I like him fine. He's a good doctor, a tremendous hard worker.'

'I like him too. But he's not like us. He's a driven man, Carly. Nothing will put him off from what he thinks he has to do.' A brief pause and then, 'He'll let no one stand in his way.'

'Are you warning me, big brother?'

'I guess I am. I'm fond of my little sister, I want her to be happy.'

They drove on in silence for a minute or two longer and then she said, 'You're happy with Miranda. And think of the troubles you two went through.'

Another pause. 'Yes indeed,' he said at last. 'Yes indeed.'

Then both of them were silent.

He was the last person she had expected to call that evening. Of course, it wasn't too late; she wasn't going to go to bed for quite a while. But after the hard day he must have had, she didn't anticipate a call from Alex.

When they met usually she was expecting to see him. And, expecting him, she could control that shiver of excitement, that slight increase in her pulse rate that he always produced in her. But now he had phoned her, totally without warning. And her body warmed at the mere thought of him.

'Carly? It's Alex. I'm sorry to phone you so late; you aren't in bed, are you?'

In bed? The very thought of Alex and bed made her feel even warmer. But somehow she managed to be cool, businesslike. 'No, I'm not in bed. What can I do for you, Alex?'

'You remember I lent you a couple of articles from an American magazine about MRSA?'

'Yes, they're here on my desk.'

'Well, sorry, but I need to look at them tonight. I'm preparing a lecture. If you're not in bed, could I come round and pick them up? I could be there in ten minutes.'

'Of course you can come round, no problem,' she said without hesitation. 'Shall I put the kettle on? Fancy a cup of tea?'

'If you don't mind. I'm still a bit over-excited from my performance this evening. Need to calm down.' He rang off.

Carly stood still a moment, the phone clenched in her hand. Was this story of needing the articles just a ruse, just a means of getting into her flat late at night? She decided not. Alex was too direct, too proud to try anything like that. If he had wanted anything other than the articles he would have asked straight out. But still…why was she feeling apprehensive?

When she had come back from the lecture she had changed out of her smart suit and was now wearing comfortable, hanging out at home clothes. An ancient T-shirt, a faded pair of jeans. Ought she to change? No, this was her house; he could take her as he found her. She went to put the kettle on anyway.

He arrived in his stated ten minutes and she was waiting to let him in. Like her, he had changed out of his formal clothes and was now in black shirt and trousers. He still looked good. 'Carly, I'm sorry to bother you at this time but I…'

'Come in. You're no bother at all.'

It was the first time he had ever been to her flat. He stood in the centre of the living room, looked round. It was a small flat, a small living room. He seemed to make the place look even smaller. And he looked at her.

She picked up the folder with the articles in,

made to offer it to him. But then somehow it slipped from her hand, the papers inside fluttering to the floor.

He looked at her, she stared back. She remembered it had been like this when they had first met in the Delivery Room—or rather when they first became aware of each other as man and woman. There was no need of words. Something passed between them—a knowledge, an understanding that was too deep for language.

She held out her arms, a gesture half of surrender, half of invitation. And then she sighed as he moved to her, took her, wrapped his arms round her and brought his mouth down to hers in a soul-wrenching kiss.

He was the master. One arm clutched her to him, pulled her against him so that her womanly curves moulded against the muscles of his body. The other hand cradled her head, held her prisoner so that she should not escape his kisses.

She didn't want to escape. She revelled in his mastery, happy to submit to him, to offer him all that he could demand. Her mouth opened to let him taste her sweetness, an emblem of a yet greater sur-render that would be his if he desired it.

A tiny corner of her mind surveyed what was happening in wonderment. This was not the cautious Carly, the woman who had been hurt before and had vowed never to be hurt again. This was a woman hurling towards total aban-donment. What was she doing?

But most of her knew. Body and spirit, she was his, to command as he wished. Never had she felt such power in a man. And never had she wished so wholeheartedly to please him.

The kiss lasted…a minute, ten minutes, an hour? She didn't know. But when eventually he loosened his hold on her, led her, her feet stum-bling, to sit beside him on the couch, she knew that for her the world would never be the same again.

For a while they lay there, slumped together. Her head was on his shoulder, her hand on his chest, and she could feel his madly beating heart. Just like hers, in fact.

She wondered what he would do next. What they would do next. Whatever, he must decide.

Suddenly he spoke. It sounded like *'Chyort'*. And it didn't sound very nice.

'What did you say?' she muttered.

'It was a Russian word. Not a very polite one.'

'It didn't sound very polite. Alex, why are you swearing?'

He sighed. Under her hand she felt his chest rise, his lungs take a giant gasp of air and then breathe it out. 'I kissed you,' he said. 'I didn't intend to. I didn't come here to kiss you. I genuinely came to pick up the folder. And then I…'

'Alex! Whatever you did, I did it with you, consciously and very happily.' She paused a moment and then said, softly, 'And it was like nothing that has ever happened to me before.'

'Nor me,' he said after a while. 'Carly, now I think that I was going mad. For a while there was no time, only you and me and the world contracted so that only we were in it. But the world isn't like that.'

'You're telling me we have to go back into the real world?' Her voice was pained.

'It's the one we live in,' he said flatly.

'So where do we go now?'

'Carly, my life is not my own. You know that. I've made no secret of the fact that I must go back to Nyrova. That is my hospital; I have to run it. And there is no place for you there.'

The sheer wonder of the kiss was ebbing now; it was hard for her, but she was being dragged back into the real world. Alex was telling her of his problems. Well, she had her own ghosts too. Her past was catching up on her, her previous caution reasserting itself.

'What are you trying to tell me?' she asked. And then, 'Don't worry about hurting me. I've been hurt before and I can take it.'

Then she winced. That had slipped out; she hadn't meant to say it. And now he was looking at her with that alert look that said that he had heard what she said—and was thinking about it. 'You've been hurt before?'

She dismissed his question. 'Everyone gets hurt at some time or other; forget that I said that.'

Now they were silent together. His arm was

still round her shoulder; she still held his hand. The kiss was now a memory. But she knew it was one she would never forget. Eventually, 'So what do we do now?' she asked.

He frowned. She could see him thinking, considering. 'Whatever is between us will have to be short. In three months we must part. You will stay here, I will go back to my hospital. Perhaps we could have an affair—something we both know would be short-lived. But I know you wouldn't want that—and neither would I.'

She was curious. 'You're right, I wouldn't want an affair. But why wouldn't you?'

'I'd be scared of falling fully in love with you. And that I don't…can't…want.'

'Right. So it's still the same question. What do we do now?'

'Can we carry on as before? First for purely practical reasons—we work well together. Second because…because I don't want to be parted from you completely. You may not be my lover but…but I would like to dream.'

She took his arm from round her shoulders

and stepped forward to collect the papers that had spilled out of the folder. Then she handed the folder to him. 'Here you are,' she said. 'I don't know whether to call you lover or dream lover. I'll see you in our room on Monday morning. Now you'd better go. I've had a hard day.'

She put out her hand and he shook it. 'Goodnight, Carly,' he said. 'I would have liked things to be different.' And he was gone.

Carly had a hot bath, made herself a malted milk drink and went to bed. Within minutes she was asleep. She had felt, thought, enough for one day. Mind and body both needed escape.

On Monday morning they had arranged to meet in the room they were to share. Carly set off extra early, hoping to be there before him, hoping to have established herself in the room so she could greet him just as an ordinary colleague.

She walked past cleaning staff, polishing, vacuuming. She'd decided. Saturday night was to be—not forgotten, but not referred to. Not for a while anyway. Today they would be medical colleagues.

She should have known better. Alex was already in the room. From the papers scattered across his desk and the pages of notes he was taking, he had been there quite some time. She hadn't expected to see him; for a moment she was shocked.

He smiled, came from behind the desk towards her, arms outstretched. Then he caught himself, frowned and lowered his arms.

Her decision, her previous determination was forgotten. She stepped forward, gave him a quick kiss on the lips.

'After Saturday night we both know that things will never be the same as they were,' she said. 'We mean something to each other, but I'm still not sure what. I don't know you, Alex, and there is so much I want, I need, to know. But for now we'll have to see what happens. Today and the rest of the week, we'll just work like ordinary doctors. Of course, if you want, you can tell me that nothing did happen and I'll never mention it again.'

For a moment his face was blank—and then he smiled. Stepping forward, he picked her up, gave her a bear hug, lifted her just as he had John. He kissed her quickly and then set her down again. 'There is something,' he said. 'I try never to lie to myself—though sometimes it is hard. But you are right. There must be something between us. What it will be, I don't know. But it is there.'

Quietly, Carly heaved a great sigh of relief. She knew she had to make this offer to Alex. Desperately she had hoped he would not accept.

She said, 'So I guess we will…'

The new phone rang. Both looked at it. 'We can't have a love life and work,' Carly said dolefully, picking up the receiver. 'Is it always going to be like this?'

'Guess so,' Alex said, equally gloomily.

It was an SHO who was on duty at A and E. 'We're a bit busy,' he said, 'and I could do with a hand. Ambulance has just arrived; there's an RTA has been brought in. Female, stepped into the road, knocked down by a slow-moving car. Paramedics say it's not too serious, no bad bleeds, no apparently broken bones. Just bruises, abrasions, a bad cut on her leg. But she's in shock and she's very worried. She's thirty-two weeks pregnant.'

'Any signs of labour starting?' Carly asked.

'Not so far. But that doesn't mean that it won't start.'

'True. Well, if the injuries aren't too serious we'll let you get her stabilised first, suture the cuts and so on. Then we'll come down and check that all's well with the baby. If there's any suggestion of labour you're to bleep me at once. We'll probably admit her later. Just overnight.'

'Sounds like a plan.'

It was a plan that worked perfectly. Alex finished his note-taking, then accompanied Carly down to A and E. The SHO had done a good job of calming the woman, persuading her that relaxing, trying not to worry, was the best possible thing for her unborn child. But Mrs Green was still relieved to see the two baby-specialist doctors.

Carly motioned for Alex to deal with the

woman. There was a fact that had to be faced. It didn't irritate her any more. She understood it, but it seemed a bit unfair. Alex was better at calming his patients than she was. He seemed to radiate authority, to inspire instant and absolute confidence. Perhaps it was his size; perhaps it was his deep voice; perhaps it was the fact that when faced with babies, or pregnant women, or children, he just smiled more. But he had it.

Alex took the patient's hand. 'Mrs Green, the doctor you have just seen has assured us that there's nothing seriously wrong with you. You had a lucky escape, but that's over now. I gather your husband has been informed and he's coming in to see you. What I want to do with Dr Sinclair here is just check on the baby and then we're going to admit you overnight. There's nothing wrong, you understand. This is just a precaution.'

'Of course, Doctor,' Mrs Green said.

'Now, I'd just like to listen to your baby's heart,' Alex said. 'See how well…' He paused. 'Do you know if you're having a little boy or a little girl?'

'A boy. My husband wanted to know, though he didn't care which it was to be.'

'The best attitude. Do you have a name yet?'

'Two names. Martin James. We're trying to please both grandfathers.'

'They'll be pleased just to have a grandchild. Now, Nurse, if you'll prepare Mrs Green I'll…' Alex bent over the curved abdomen, carefully placed his stethoscope and then smiled. 'That is perfect,' he said. 'A good strong heartbeat. Mrs Green, you're going to have a tough little boy. Now, we need just one more check; we'd like you to have a scan. Then you can be admitted to the ward and have a sleep.'

He turned, raised his eyes at Carly. 'You see to the scan and then go up to the ward and fill in all the paperwork,' she said. 'I'll hold the fort here.'

'Sounds good. I'll arrange a trolley to the scan.'

Carly sighed when he had gone. She loved watching him work.

Mrs Green was wheeled away, Alex going with

her. Carly walked outside to discover that the A
and E Department had suddenly gone into over-
drive. Sometimes it happened like this; it didn't
have to be a Saturday night or the result of a fire
or a massive RTA. Just that more people
suddenly needed attention. Carly stood for a
moment, aware that what seemed like confusion
around her was actually well-organised. Or as
well-organised as it could be. One of the quickly
moving passing A and E consultants stopped for
a minute and said, 'Carly, doing anything right
now? Help us for a second?'

'Happy to. So long as I can get away if any of
my special cases come in.' She had been co-
opted like this in the past.

'Woman in cubicle F. Not serious, I don't
think. If it is, give me a yell. Otherwise bandage,
calming, cup of tea and discharge.'

'Makes your job sound easy,' she said with a
grin.

A thin, shabbily dressed woman was lying on
the trolley in cubicle F. Mrs Roberts had given
her age as thirty-five but she looked much older.

'Mrs Roberts had a fall at home,' the nurse in the cubicle said. 'She has a badly bruised face and her arm and shoulder hurt where she fell on them. Her side hurts too.'

Carly looked at Mrs Roberts's inflamed face and then at the nurse. The nurse was behind Mrs Roberts and couldn't be seen. She looked back at Carly and shrugged. Both knew that Mrs Roberts had not fallen. She had been struck—violently. This was a domestic. They were always hard to deal with.

'The nurse will help you get undressed, Mrs Roberts,' Carly said gently. 'Then we'll have a look at you.'

She winced when she saw the discolouration on Mrs Roberts's side and shoulder and ran her fingers as gently as she could across the bones.

'How did this happen, Mrs Roberts? It seems to be the result of more than a simple fall.'

'I fell downstairs; it's easy to do. Now, can we get on with it?'

'Well, I need to X-ray your ribs. I suspect that

at least one is broken. There's no chance that you are pregnant, is there?'

'No chance. I'm not pregnant! No doubt about that.'

'Well, I'll just go and organise the portable X-ray, then.'

She had sent for the machine and the radiographer was positioning it when Alex returned. She heard his cough outside the cubicle, realised that he would not come in unless invited. She popped her head through the curtains. 'Dr Braikovitch, I'm dealing with Mrs Roberts here. Come in, I'd welcome your opinion.'

In fact she didn't need his opinion. She wondered if he could work his usual masculine charm on Mrs Roberts. Or perhaps it only worked for those having babies, babies and children.

He entered the cubicle, smiled at the nurse and radiographer and looked down at Mrs Roberts. Then he frowned. 'You're not going to X-ray this patient?'

'I am. I need to know if any of her ribs are broken.' Carly's voice was curt; she didn't like her professional expertise being questioned in front of the nurse and radiographer.

'But she's…' He looked down at the patient. 'Mrs Roberts, you're pregnant, aren't you?'

'No, I'm not! I told this other doctor here and I'm telling you. I'm not pregnant!'

'Don't take any X-rays till you're told,' Alex ordered the radiographer. 'Dr Sinclair, could I have a word with you?' Without waiting for her answer, he swept aside the curtains and stepped outside.

Seething inside, Carly followed him. She thought Alex had learned, now knew how to treat his colleagues. Obviously she had been wrong. 'Well, Dr Braikovitch?' she said icily. 'You have something to say to me?'

'You don't X-ray a pregnant woman. And that woman is pregnant.'

'I asked her if she was pregnant and she assured me she was not. And I see no sign of it in her body. What makes you think she is?'

He frowned. 'There's something about the eyes, the shape of the mouth. When she moved on that mattress, her body was held in a different way—and it wasn't possible broken bones. That woman is undernourished, and you know a lot of the women that I see are undernourished too. You get a feeling for it.'

'She ought to know if she's pregnant or not!'

'She's hiding it. From herself or, more likely, from her partner. I've come across that too.'

'But if she assures me that she's not pregnant and she's expecting an X-ray now and I don't give her one…she's an awkward patient and she's going to get worse.'

'Tell her you need to do further tests. Lie to her if necessary. Take a urine sample, do an Icon test. Then you'll know for certain if she's pregnant or not and you can carry on with whatever course of action is correct. But Carly, you can't risk damaging an unborn child.'

Her shoulders slumped. 'You're right, I can't. Okay, I'll do an Icon test. But if you're wrong…'

'I might be wrong. I'd like to be wrong.' His voice was suddenly harsh. 'I recognised that bruise on the woman's face at once; I've seen enough of them in my time. It was made by a fist.

Perhaps I am wrong, perhaps my judgement was clouded. But I can guess why the woman doesn't want to admit to being pregnant. An Icon test will show what the truth is.'

'True.' She looked at him for a moment, surveyed his obdurate face. 'Alex, you just said you might be wrong. But you know you're right, don't you?'

Now he looked uneasy. 'Well, I could be right or wrong. But since I've met you I've tried to be a bit less…forceful in my opinions. You're teaching me patience. I suspect it's something I need. In fact you're teaching me many things.'

There was just time for them to look at each other in a very non-medical way, to consider exactly what he might have meant by this. But they were still both doctors in a busy A and E ward. After a moment he shook his head, as if to rid himself of thoughts that were too trouble-some. He said, 'I think I'd better leave the rest of this to you. I suspect that it's going to be more than a simple medical case and you might need to involve Social Services, perhaps even the police. And that's all new to me.'

'You're probably right. Alex, thanks for spotting that that woman was pregnant. I would have hated to…'

'No doctor ever gets everything right—we all make mistakes. The good thing is when you have colleagues who can help or support you.'

There was something about the flat way he said this that made her wonder if he was thinking about some episode in his past. 'You don't have much support at your hospital, do you?' she asked.

'My other two doctors are hardworking; they do what they can. But they are young. They will learn and inevitably they learn from me rather than I learn from them.' Then he smiled. 'Now, Dr Sinclair, I believe you have a patient waiting. And I don't envy your having to deal with her.'

'Thanks for your support,' she said.

It had started as a favour to a colleague and was technically nothing to do with her. But it was two hours before Carly could feel that she had done everything that she ought and press on with her own work. She finally caught up with Alex at the end of the morning. They went into the doctors' room and managed to share a drink.

'You were right—Mrs Roberts was pregnant,' she told him. 'But I'm still not sure how you knew. As well as the bruises and lacerations on her face, she had fractures of the humerus and two ribs. We sent for the orthopaedics consultant in time. Then she was persuaded to make an official complaint against her husband so we had to involve Social Services and the police.'

'She claimed she wasn't pregnant because she didn't want to be pregnant,' Alex guessed. 'She was trying to hide it from herself.'

'True.' She looked at him thoughtfully. 'Do you get many cases like that in your own hospital, Alex?'

He shook his head. 'My people tend to have large families. Unfortunately, a large proportion of them die. We try, we try desperately, to get the death rate down, and I think we're having some success. But it's never enough!'

'After the lecture last Saturday you promised

me you'd tell me more about your work and your home,' she said. 'I'd really like that.'

'Why? Are you just curious?'

He looked at her as if her reply was important. And it was, of course. She decided to be honest—even if it meant revealing a little more of herself than she had intended. 'I am curious. But I want to know you better. And I think that I'll never understand you unless I know something of your background.'

'That's true of most people. Why pick on me?'

'Because you're not like most people. And be-cause…there's that something between us.'

He said nothing to this.

CHAPTER FIVE

IT WAS one of those desk jobs. Hard, boring but
necessary. As well as acting as Alex's junior, Carly
still had some duties in the department as a whole.

She had been asked to look through the
previous six months' take-up of drugs, check
what was still available and decide if orders had
to be changed for the next six months. 'When I
started medicine we just ordered what we liked,'
John had told her. 'But then they let accountants
into the business. And now I spend as much time
adding up money as I do taking pulses. You can
do the same.' So she sat in the corner of her
office and settled down to work.

It wasn't clinical medicine but Alex had
offered to help her. And to her surprise he was
wonderful at the job. 'If you've ever dealt with

Soviet bureaucracy,' he told her, 'then this is child's play. And I want to feel envious at the supplies you can order so easily.' So the work she had expected to take the entire afternoon was over in a couple of hours.

She beamed at him. 'Now I know I'm glad that you came,' she said. 'You've saved me hours of tedious checking and re-checking. Come on, if you've got the makings in that big bag of yours, I'll make you some of your black tea. And double chocolate biscuits on me.'

'Sounds like a feast. And the doctors' room should be deserted now.' He paused a moment and then said, 'I have something to show you, I think.'

'You only think you have something to show me? Now that is intriguing. Something in that bag?'

'Let's go for that tea.'

To show solidarity with him—and because she was getting quite a taste for it herself—she made black tea for them both. Then they sat side by side on a couch, the coffee table in front of them.

Their shoulders, thighs, hands touched from time to time. She wondered if, when it happened, he got the same tiny thrill as she did.

He opened his bag, took out an envelope. 'I brought these to show members of MedAsia just where their aid was going. The place I work in is a place of great beauty but also much poverty. The land is hard. Pitilessly hot in summer, terribly cold in winter. The people there are tough; they don't take easily to discipline. Perhaps because of this, they suffered under Soviet rule.'

He handed her a set of pictures. 'These are photographs of some of the local people.'

Carly looked, fascinated, at the pictures. 'Their faces are fierce,' she said, 'but they seem to smile a lot.'

'They are fierce. The land has been swept by conquerors again and again. Some of these people are the descendants of Genghis Khan's Golden Horde, who terrorised Western Europe in the thirteenth century.'

'So what is it like giving these people medical treatment?'

He grinned. 'You've probably guessed. You have to let them know who's boss. They don't like people who can't make up their minds. They know what they want and they go for it with little thought of the consequences. And they want to know the truth. If a man—or a woman—is going to die, then you tell them. And they accept it.'

Carly shivered. 'It sounds…very honest and straightforward,' she said, 'but…'

'It is the way we live.'

'The way we live? We? Are you like that, Alex? Is it the way for a doctor to behave?'

He frowned. 'You must remember that medicine here is not the same as medicine there. I must do the best I can with the limited resources I have and the often awkward patients that I get. If sometimes I trample over what Westerners might call people's rights—well, too bad. I do what I have to do.'

It was obvious that he now wanted to talk about something else. 'Here, this is a photograph of my hospital.'

She looked at what seemed to be a collection

of wooden shacks, with a great radio antennae rising from the roof of one.

'It's made of wood?'

'An excellent insulator in winter and summer. Wood should be used more as a building material. You just have to be careful about fires.'

'I'll bet,' she said.

The next picture showed sets of low hills rolling off to distant white-capped mountains. It was a desolate landscape, but she could see its attraction. 'And this is a typical landscape?'

'Typical,' he said. He was looking at the picture with an expression of…doubt?

'It seems as if this means something special to you?'

When she looked at him his eyes had a distant ironic look, as if he was seeing something that both entranced and repelled him. 'It does mean something special to me. Carly, all this land right up to the foothills of those mountains…' His voice trailed away.

'Yes?' She felt as though he was about to tell her something that might make his enigmatic personality a little more understandable. 'Alex, what about all the land up to the foothills?'

'It all belonged to my great-grandfather.'

'It what?'

'It was part of the family estate. A hundred years ago my family owned land practically as far as the eye could see. My great-grandfather was Duke of Nyrova.'

'Duke?' Carly was having difficulty in taking this in. 'Your great-grandfather? Does that mean that you're a duke too? I've never talked to a duke. In fact I've never met one.'

He smiled. 'All aristocratic titles were abolished after the 1917 revolution. There are no more Russian dukes. In fact this land was given to one of my ancestors by the tsar in the sixteenth century, as a reward for being a great soldier. But the land he was given was as far from Moscow as possible. That meant he was likely to be less of a troublemaker.'

'Some family traits carry on, don't they?' Carly muttered.

He put another photograph in front of her, this

time of a large building, gutted by fire. 'The ancestral home,' he said. 'Burned down by Russian troops in 1918 after the revolution. Technically, I suppose, the land is now mine.'

Carly nodded. 'I've wondered why you aren't working in Moscow or even somewhere in the rest of Europe. Or you'd easily get a job in America; you could be an immensely successful surgeon. But you've decided to go back to where your family came from, to practise medicine in a place where your talents are wasted. You feel you owe the people there something, don't you?'

He shrugged. 'It wasn't entirely a good thing when the old USSR fell apart in 1991. Many of the outlying regions, outlying republics—they found themselves worse off than under Soviet rule. Nyrova and its surrounding area was one. My great-grandfather had the power of life or death over his peasants. He was an autocrat but he also felt responsibility for his people. Perhaps I feel a little the same way.'

'I see,' said Carly. There were a thousand questions she had to ask but first she had to get used to the idea of Alex being a duke—even if the title had been abolished. It ought not to make any difference. But somehow it did.

'Perhaps, after I have gone back, you would like to visit me,' Alex suggested. 'There are two months in spring and two months in autumn when the country is truly beautiful. You could see where I work, how I work. And perhaps then you would understand a little more.'

'Understand your work—or you?'

His answer was simple and Carly thought it forbidding. 'I am my work. I think of little else.'

Then he said something that made her heart leap. 'Until I met you,' he said.

There was silence for a moment. She looked at him, unsure of what to say next. He looked perplexed—which was unusual for him. But why shouldn't he be perplexed? She wasn't sure what to make of the situation herself.

'I keep on thinking that I'm a doctor, I've got my work to do, I'm enjoying it,' she said quietly. 'That I just don't need…need…emotional entanglement.'

A wry smile. 'Is that what I am? An emotional entanglement?'

She had to smile herself. 'Not much of a phrase, is it? But I can't think of a better one. Alex, I just don't know what to do about you. I feel that I've got this great…' She tried but she just couldn't bring herself to say the word. Love? Was what she felt love? She just didn't know.

She started again, more cautiously this time. 'I *think* I've got this great feeling for you. But it frightens me. And I don't know what to do.' She looked at him, her face forlorn. 'Alex, I feel I'm stripping my soul naked here for you and it hurts. You've got to say something back.'

His voice was low. 'You say you just don't know what to do about me. That's not my trouble; I do know what I have to do about you. I have to remember that I am needed at my hospital. I have no time for…for… romantic interludes and so I must tell you, as kindly as I can, that there can be no future for us.'

'Well, that's plain enough,' she said.

'It's too plain!' For the first time ever she heard

him raise his voice. 'I said that I knew what I had to do! But Carly, I just can't do it! Me, the hard, tough, iron man. I just can't let you go, not as casually as that. And I…'

And then, as ever, rescue from their torment came from the most obvious source. The door opened and Alice peered in. 'Got a minute, either of you?' she asked. 'I've got a problem with a child with an advanced case of the wriggles. I need to give him an injection and he just won't keep still. There's his mother, the nurse and me and we just can't pin him down.'

'I'll come,' said Alex. 'Wriggling children are one of my specialities.'

'And I'll come and watch,' said Carly. 'I haven't seen a good wrestling match for a while.'

She knew that the conversation with Alex was not over. Too much had been said and much more needed to be said. But it couldn't be said now. She'd be content just being in the same room as him. Even if they were working, they would be together.

* * *

John had changed Alex's timetable slightly and asked him to work, still with Carly, on A and E for two days out of five. The normal Senior Registrar was off work having a knee replaced.

There was the usual influx of cases, trivial, problematic and serious. A little girl who had pushed three beads into her ear—with skill and luck Carly managed to get them out. An eight-month-old baby whose temperature had soared—admitted at once for treatment. A nine-year-old boy who had tripped playing football and now was in pain and couldn't walk. X-rays showed a greenstick fracture so Carly sent him off for plastering.

And Alex was busy too. Occasionally they passed in the corridor with time for nothing but a quick smile. Situation normal.

In the middle of the afternoon, quite independently, they had both decided to grab a quick drink. There wasn't even time to sit down; they stood, mugs in hand, and exchanged brief words about what they had done so far that day. The morning's conversation was not referred to; this was not the time. And then Jack came in the room.

'Caught you both,' he said. 'That's great. Alex, we're having a tiny get-together at my house on Saturday night with the rest of the family and wondered if you'd like to come for supper. You'll know Carly and Toby, of course, and you'll be able to meet my wife Miranda and Toby's wife Annie. They've heard all about you and would love to meet you.'

There was the quickest of glances towards Carly and then Alex said, 'I'd love to. It will be nice to socialise with my colleagues outside of the hospital.'

'Good. You will be able to come, won't you, Carly?'

She looked at her brother thoughtfully. This wasn't an unusual invitation; the three of them were very close. But why invite Alex? She knew they got on well, but still… Did Jack have some ulterior motive? Oh, well, what if he did? 'I'd love to come too,' she said.

'Settled, then. Arrive about eight?' And Jack was gone.

'We could go together if you like,' Carly offered. 'Shall I pick you up?'

'I would like for us to go together. But I will pick you up.'

She grinned. 'Do you think it's a man's job to drive—not a woman's?'

He grinned back. 'I think that exactly. I won't apologise for it, that's the way I am.'

'I've noticed,' she said.

When he picked her up on Saturday evening there was a sheaf of flowers in the back of the car—a carefully wrapped bundle of red roses.

'Roses are a Russian flower,' he told her. 'Round the seas to the south of my country there are fields and fields of them.'

He reached for the sheaf, carefully took out a single rose and handed it to her. 'This one I wish you to have.'

'Alex, you can't take one rose out of a bunch

and give it to me! I suppose these are for Miranda—she should get the full bunch.'

He shook his head. 'There are twenty roses there; I wish to give her nineteen. In Russia, you only take an even number of flowers to a funeral. An even number symbolises death.'

She looked at him, astonished. 'Is that true?'

'If I gave an even number of flowers to someone in my town, they would be both upset and angered. It would be gross bad manners.'

'But it's just a belief—a superstition. And you are the least superstitious man I have ever met.'

'Sometimes people need irrational beliefs. They help bring order to what often seems to be a disordered world. Tell me, Carly, do you believe your future is written in the stars?'

'Certainly not!' She was indignant.

'And do you ever look in the newspaper and see what your horoscope tells you? And feel pleased if you are promised something good?'

She was silent for a moment and then said, 'Thanks for the single rose. We'll leave it in the car until you take me home.' She felt she had lost the argument.

Carly had been wondering if Miranda and Annie would take to Alex. By now, of course, she knew him, could tell what he was feeling, thinking. But other people still sometimes found him uncommunicative, even arrogant. However, her two sisters-in-law liked him at once. The roses were very welcome.

Carly had told Alex about her nieces and nephew, who were all fast asleep in the bedroom. There was Miranda and Jack's baby daughter, Esme, and Toby and Annie's newborn daughter, Lara, and Charlie, Toby's young son by his first marriage. After he'd presented the flowers, Alex also produced three carefully wrapped packages and gave one to Miranda, two to Annie. 'Not for you but for your babies,' he said. 'But you may undo them, of course.'

Carly was as intrigued as the two mothers, watching as the paper was torn aside. There were two brightly painted rattles for the younger children, a set of the traditional nesting dolls for Charlie.

'Look at the painting on this rattle,' Annie exclaimed. 'It's beautiful and it must have taken some poor soul hours to finish. No way does this get sucked to death. It's going to hang on the wall.'

Alex took it from her and shook it. 'Quite a good rattling noise, though,' he said.

Toby was examining the painting on the nest of dolls, discovering that each one was different, had a different uniform and expression. These are truly beautiful, Alex,' he said. 'Where are they from?'

'In my country, traditionally they are carved by the men and then painted by the women. They are work for winter—when it is too dark, too cold to go out.'

Miranda shook her rattle. 'Well, I'll lean over Esme's cot and rattle this to her,' she said. 'But otherwise, like Annie's, this will be hung on the wall.'

'Now we'll have a drink to celebrate,' Jack said.

It was a very enjoyable evening. After a while they were invited into the dining room, where

Miranda had put out a delicious buffet supper. Carly had filled her plate and was about to sit down when Alex said with a smile, 'You shouldn't sit there, Carly.'

She looked at him, confused. 'Why not?'

'We were talking earlier about Russian folk beliefs. One is that if a woman sits at the corner of a table she will remain single for the next seven years.'

'You don't want that, do you, Carly?' Miranda said with a giggle.

'But I wanted to sit next to the trifle. Then I could help myself to as much as I wanted without anyone noticing.'

Miranda took the trifle and replaced it to the centre of the table. 'Move,' she said. 'I'm not waiting for seven years before I get a new brother-in-law. It might be a superstition but you can't be too careful.'

The supper, as ever, was superb. They ate and chatted and Alex answered questions about medicine in Nyrova. Annie was a doctor, Miranda a midwife; they were fascinated.

After an hour or so they heard gurgling noises from the adjoining room and then the first tiny cry. 'Somebody's hungry,' Miranda said and went to feed and change Esme, while Alex chatted easily with Jack, Toby and Annie. Then Alex was invited by Annie to see Charlie and Lara, who were still sleeping soundly. Carly, of course, went too.

It was interesting to watch Alex look at children and babies who weren't ill. As a doctor, he had to maintain a professional distance, but now, Alex wasn't being a doctor. And Carly saw a different man from the tough, apparently distant man that so many people thought him to be. Alex loved children. It was obvious from the way he stroked their cheeks, gently pulled up their bedclothes, brushed their hair.

'Two lovely children,' he said. 'You must be very pleased—and proud.'

'Well, yes,' Annie said. 'You probably know Charlie is Toby's, not mine—but I still love him to bits.'

'That's obvious,' Alex said, looking from the devoted mother to her two adorable children.

They went back into the living room to find Miranda walking up and down with a fretful Esme in her arms. 'Usually she's a good baby,' Miranda said, 'but tonight she's decided to be awkward. Is there a particular Russian way for calming babies, Alex?'

'Noisy babies are universal. As is the way of calming them.'

'Calming them? Do you want to try with this one?' Miranda asked.

Carly could see the joy in his eyes as he said, 'I should love to try.'

He held baby Esme with such care and tenderness. He walked her up and down, rocking her gently with obvious expertise. But he couldn't stop that tiny wail.

'Alex, you're a failure,' Carly said with a grin. 'I had thought the Russian method might be superior—but it's not. That baby is not going to stop crying. What are you going to do? What else would you do in Russia?'

'Sing to her,' said Alex.

'Well, go on, then. Sing to her.' It was meant

as a joke, not as a challenge. But he looked round and she saw that he was seriously thinking about it. 'If you want to, that is,' she added.

'Perhaps people might not want to hear my voice.'

'If it'll get the baby to sleep you can sing as out of tune as you like,' Miranda said. 'This is now a baby-centred household.'

'I could sing her a rugby song,' Toby offered. 'You go first, Alex, and then Jack and I will try. Prove that we men do have our uses.'

'Very well,' said Alex.

Carly loved Alex's voice. It was deep, musical. There was a fascinating edge to it that suggested that, no matter how skilful a speaker he might be, English was not his native tongue. Every time he spoke she felt that little thrill of excitement. And now he was going to sing! She had never thought of him singing.

He started, sang quietly; he was trying to lull a baby to sleep. And his voice was as soft, as seductive as anything that Carly had ever heard. He might be trying to make the baby sleep. But to

Carly the sounds conjured up quite a different scene. This was a love song. She glanced quickly at Miranda, at Annie. She could tell that they felt the same way, this was a love song. But she felt that Alex was singing to her, not to them. Or was he singing to the baby?

She wasn't even surprised when he stopped singing and showed them that the baby was asleep. That voice could make anyone do anything. Gently, carefully, he handed Esme over to her mother. 'That was lovely and we'd all clap,' Miranda whispered to him. 'But now she's asleep I'd like to keep her that way.'

'That song was so beautiful,' Carly said when Miranda was safely out of the room. 'What was it called? And what is it all about?'

'It's a folk song called My Two Stars. It's hard to translate—it wouldn't make much sense in English—but it's about a man who is walking home through a forest. He's tired and he has a long way to go and he's not even sure he's on the right path. But every now and then there's a break in the trees overhead and he can see two stars. The two stars guide him—and he thinks one is his wife and the other is his baby daughter. They are both beautiful and he loves them both and they are the things that make his life worthwhile. So, although his life is hard, he is happy and he sings to his wife and daughter.' A brief pause and then Alex went on, 'He is a lucky man.'

It was said in the same casual way that he had been speaking so far. But Carly wondered if she could hear a change in tone, a suggestion that Alex might almost be envious of the man in the woods. She was imagining things!

It was nearly time to go. Carly knew just how tiring very young children could be, how sleep become something to be missed and longed for. So she had arranged with Alex that they would leave quite early. And when she suggested that this was about the time to leave, neither Toby nor Jack objected very hard.

'Our turn to be at home next,' Annie said as they left. 'Alex, you'll come to us with Carly, won't you?'

'I would be very pleased to. I don't have a family myself, so it's nice to visit other people's.'

And so they left. 'Nice, my family, aren't they?' Carly asked as he drove her home.

'Very nice. And one of the nicest things about them is that they appear to realise how very very lucky they are.'

'You'd like a family yourself?' Carly asked, greatly daring.

His voice was cold, remote, as he answered her. 'I have a hospital to run. That is my family.'

She decided to ignore his coolness, thinking that he was trying to avoid having a further conversation about their future. Well, too bad. That was something that still had to come. But when they were both ready.

Casually, she said, 'I've learned quite a lot about being Russian this evening. You told me about the flowers, you told me not to sit at the corner of the table, you sang to the baby in Russian.'

'I hope I didn't bore people. Sometimes I get the urge to explain things and…'

'Just the opposite! Learning about where you've come from, the kind of things you believe, it makes me feel I know you better. And I like you more for it. Just think—if you hadn't told me, I might have remained single for the next seven years.'

'True. That would be terrible,' he said.

She couldn't make out whether he was joking or not. So she decided to say nothing.

CHAPTER SIX

IT WAS still quite early when Alex drew up outside her flat. Especially for a Saturday night when they didn't have to work the next day. Under their rotation they were entitled to one complete weekend off in every four. The younger doctors looked forward to the free weekend with excitement, spent much of their time planning what they were going to do. Usually Carly wasn't bothered. Saturday night was like any other night. But tonight seemed to be different.

She had been wondering about this, thinking about arguments for and arguments against all the way home. So much so that Alex must have found her a poor conversationalist. But now they were outside her flat and Alex was opening his door and she had to decide so…

The question came without any conscious decision on her part. 'It's still quite early, Alex. Would you like to come in for a nightcap?' Her voice sounded quite calm, she was surprised.

He didn't reply at once, instead closing the car door and turning to look at her. 'You want me to come in for a nightcap?'

She knew what he was asking, knew that she was taking a momentous decision. 'Yes,' she said.

'Then I should very much like to have a nightcap with you. I think this has been the most pleasant evening I have spent since I came to England. It would be a pity if it ended so soon.'

'The most pleasant evening of all?'

'All except one,' he said. 'The evening I spent with you. And that evening I have tried to forget—without much success.'

'Some nights just turn out to be magic,' she said. 'Usually the ones not planned in advance.'

She took the red rose he had given her and led him to her front door.

Unusually, her flat was in a bit of a mess; she hadn't intended to invite anyone back. She had tried three dresses on and rejected two, which were still tossed carelessly over the back of her couch. Hastily she grabbed them, ran into the bedroom and threw them on the bed. Then she told him to sit while she put her red rose into water.

'Miranda was delighted with her odd number of flowers,' she called from the kitchen, 'and I'm delighted with my single rose. Would you like a glass of red wine?'

'I'd love one.'

She had noticed that although he had been offered more than one, he had only had a single drink at Jack's. She brought in two full glasses of red wine, and the red rose in its cut glass vase. The vase went on to the coffee table in front of them and she offered him his wine. 'You didn't drink much at Jack's,' she said. 'I thought Russians were supposed to be big drinkers.'

'Many are big drinkers. And heavy smokers. In the town I come from, smoking and drinking is the easiest way to get over the sadness of life, especially in winter. But if you spend any time at the emergency department—what you call

A and E—you soon discover that this escape is a hard-earned pleasure.'

'So you don't drink to excess?'

'Never.'

She took up her glass, clinked it against his. 'You told me that Russians loved toasts. So here's to us. But don't throw it back in one.'

'I shall sip. I am sure this wine deserves it. The company certainly does.'

Carly sipped her own wine, sighed and leaned back on the couch. 'I love being with my family,' she said, 'and I'm so pleased that you liked them and they liked you. You seemed like one of the group.'

'Almost,' he agreed. 'You are a happy family. Three children, all healthy—it must be a great joy.'

'I love them to bits,' she said. 'And perhaps one day I'll…' She decided not to go there, be happy with what she had already. And this evening was going well. She had brought him to her flat hoping that they could talk, perhaps she could learn a little more about him. She was conscious that the last time they had been here—the night he had described as magic—had been unfinished business. She wanted, she needed to know more about him.

She felt happy. And because she was happy she leaned over and kissed him gently on the lips. He accepted the kiss and in his turn he kissed her. Also on the lips. But not quite so gently.

Perhaps it had been the wrong thing to do. Afterwards she wondered—had she really acted in such a forward manner? It didn't seem forward at the time—it seemed proper and pleasant. And very enjoyable. She kissed him again, a third kiss. Or did he kiss her? She wasn't sure. It was so obvious that it was something that they both wanted. It seemed to last a bit longer than the previous two. A bit longer than she had intended. Only then did she realise how much she wanted him to kiss her. She wanted even more than that too.

Now his arms were round her, his body pressed hers back against the couch; he knew that this was what she wanted and he wanted it too. She clutched him to her, pulled him closer.

And all the feelings that she had tried to hide came raging to the surface. She had been wrong to try and fool herself. She could not forget the last kiss. Neither could he.

For perhaps five minutes they lay there, kissing passionately, both feeling the mounting need inside them. Both knew that this would not end merely in a kiss. Both wanted— needed—more.

He released her, stood, for a moment looked down on her. She stared at his face, reading there that now there was no going back. This was what he wanted and he was determined to take it.

He bent, picked her up bodily, swung her into his arms. She marvelled at his strength as he carried her across the living room, kicked open her bedroom door and laid her tenderly on the bed. Her two dresses were thrown carelessly on to the floor. He leaned over her, kissed her again. Then he stood back and Carly heard one word form unwillingly—her own name. 'Carly?'

She knew it was a question and that after her answer there would be no turning back. But she also knew that she needed him as much as he needed her. 'Yes, Alex, please. Yes, Alex, I want you to love me.'

The emotions inside her were pent-up, demanding expression. Like a volcano she had to have release.

They both knew that now there was no time for delicate caresses, a long drawn out lovemaking. This was to be the answer to a desperate raw craving. Something between them they had tried to hide but which was now forcing its way into the open. He pulled aside her blouse, unhooked her bra and his lips descended on each pink tip in turn, both now painfully hard with desire.

The feeling of his urgency only made her more desperate herself. She didn't know how it had happened. She didn't undress herself—he must have done it. But, almost to her surprise, she found herself naked. She wanted her body to be his, to offer it, whatever he wanted he could take.

She saw that he was nearly naked too and in the midst of her abandonment a tiny worry intruded itself. 'Alex... Have you?... Not without...'

His voice was hoarse as he replied. 'All will be well; you will be safe with me.'

It didn't then take long. His body was on hers, her body reaching out to take him, welcome him to that most wonderful of havens. She could feel his strength, his need—it matched hers. And then a wondrous joint climax that seemed to go on and on, to last for ever until she thought her body could take no more and she screamed in ecstasy, hearing his voice calling too.

Then there was peace. She felt the sweat cooling on their bodies, the thumping of both their hearts declining. She rested on the curve of his arm, reached out to turn off the bedside light as they both drifted off to sleep. 'Alex?' she murmured sleepily. 'What does *ya tebya lyublyu* mean? I heard you say something like that as we...you know...'

He paused before answering. Then, 'It's Russian for "I love you".'

'Oh,' she said softly. 'And I love you too,

Alex.' Just before unconsciousness took her, she had one last thought. For the first time in a very long time, she was happy. She was content.

Some hours later she woke. It was still the middle of the night and the room was dark. She could hear, feel rustling and when she stretched out her arm Alex wasn't there.

'Alex? Are you getting dressed? You don't have to go.'

'I think I do,' he said. 'If I stayed longer I'd never move out.'

He bent over her, kissed her—but on the forehead. 'You gave me something so wonderful,' he said, 'but I must go. Carly, you know this has changed things. But how I don't yet know.' His voice was anxious.

'I know things have changed, and soon I suppose we'll have to have another sad talk about what we are to do and what is possible and have we made a terrible mistake. But for now I have another memory that I'll never forget. Alex, you know we're not just friends any more?'

'We're not?' He sounded uncertain.

'No. Are you happy with that?'

He kissed her again. 'I am happy,' he said.

She did little that Sunday, after he had gone. She rose late and cooked herself a large and leisurely breakfast. Then she unhooked her phone, turned off her mobile. This was a day to be spent entirely for herself. After a long bath she spent hours reading and listening to music. Or just lying on her couch, a half smile on her face. From time to time she reached for her single red rose and took it out of its vase to smell it. The smell was faint but still there.

In the afternoon she went for a short walk, visited the local corner shop and bought herself a large and expensive box of chocolates. Then she went home to eat them. As she went to bed that night she realised that it was the only day she could remember for months in which she had done absolutely no work. And she was happy about it.

Monday morning was to be a work day. And

before she went to work Alex phoned her. 'I don't really like phones,' he said. 'If you can't see the person you're talking to, then it's all too easy to get the wrong message.'

'That's interesting,' she said. 'I've never thought about it, but I guess it's true. So why are you phoning me now, Alex? No, that's the wrong message! I'm glad that you phoned and it's good to hear your voice.'

She heard him laugh. 'I wanted desperately to phone you or to call on you yesterday,' he said. 'But I didn't. I thought you might need time— time to think about what happened, to try to decide what you wanted to happen next.'

'That was thoughtful of you. But Alex, I've a confession. I did nothing yesterday but laze and feel happy and now I feel better for it.'

He laughed again. 'What a brilliant way to spend a day. Perhaps I ought to try to prescribe it for busy doctors.'

'So I take it you spent the day in a different way?'

'Well, I was certainly happy. But I thought and I worried and I wondered about things.'

'I didn't think, worry or wonder. I was just happy.'

'The way to be. But Carly, when we meet next, in a few minutes, it'll have to be work as usual. Back to the real world of A and E. For a while, at least.'

She sighed. 'I suppose so. But Alex, on Saturday we went beyond reality, didn't we?'

'I guess we did,' he said. 'And things will never be the same for me again.'

Sister Geraldine O'Brian, as she proudly told everyone, was a nurse of the old school. She believed in hierarchies. She was experienced, dedicated, unmarried, a stickler for the rules and the scourge of the younger nurses. She was a very skilful nurse but she had to be handled delicately.

She had just returned from a fortnight's holiday. And, having returned, she would be anxious to be certain that standards hadn't slipped in her absence.

Carly winced when she saw her. It struck her that she should have warned Alex about

Geraldine O'Brian. Alex's determination to do what was right at once would not sit easily with the Sister's belief that a good department was one that followed all the rules to the letter. Still…

'Morning, Geraldine. Good to have you back. You haven't seen the new doctor, Dr Braikovitch, have you?'

Geraldine smiled. Carly blinked. A smile so early wasn't very usual for the Sister. And Geraldine said, 'You mean Alex? We've just been dealing with a case together. He's very good, isn't he?'

'Very good,' Carly said weakly. 'Er, what kind of case?'

'Tuberculosis; I recognised it at once. I came across a dozen cases when I worked in Africa.' Geraldine sniffed. 'That young SHO said that he was just a down-and-out looking for a bed for the night. It wasn't his fault he was dirty. But I knew better and so I told Alex and, even though it wasn't a children's case, he sorted things out at once.'

'Super,' said Carly, still at a loss for words. 'So…you're looking forward to working with him?'

'Very much. That young man gets things done.'

Geraldine's eagle eye fixed on someone behind Carly's shoulder. 'Student Nurse! No matter what the hurry, you never run down the corridors in my department.'

'Probably see you later,' Carly said.

She found Alex in the A and E Doctors' Room, mug of tea in his hand. He was chatting to two younger doctors and when she came in he casually said, 'Hi, Carly,' and went on with his conversation. It seemed a bit of an anticlimax after they had meant so much to each other on Saturday night. Did they still seem so much to each other? Of course they did. In fact when she looked at him she could read his expression. The apparently absent smile for her meant so much more than it seemed. She guessed that for a while it would be better to carry on as if they were colleagues and nothing more.

'I've been talking to Sister Geraldine O'Brian,' she said. 'It looks like you've impressed her.'

'She's impressed me. She reminds me of a

couple of nurses I work with back at home. They can feel diseases, they don't have to diagnose them.' He waved to his two companions. 'I was going to talk about it to Mary and Steve here; it's a case they should study.'

'Tell me too,' said Carly.

'Well, it wasn't a paediatric case so I suppose I was interfering. But after Geraldine came to me and told me what she thought, I suspected I knew what was wrong so I acted at once. A middle-aged man came to Reception; he was dirty, poorly dressed, emaciated. Probably a vagrant of some sort. She'd seen him outside, having a last cigarette and spitting on the ground. Spitting heavily. He came in, made some vague complaint; Triage decided that he wasn't a serious case, he could wait. So he sat there a couple of minutes, coughing and spluttering. Geraldine came to take a few details from him for records, decided what was wrong and came to tell me. I took him outside, away from the other poor devils in Reception, and phoned the Infectious Diseases Registrar. He took him away at once.'

'So what was wrong with him?' asked Mary.

'He has tuberculosis. An advanced case. He would be spraying droplets all over Reception; who knows who he might have infected. So I got him out.'

'You can tell tuberculosis just by looking at a man?' Mary looked impressed.

'When you've seen as many cases as I have,' Alex said bitterly, 'then it's not very hard. And, when your supply of rifampicin is limited, then you get the chance to watch the disease progress in all its stages.'

Once the conversation was over, Carly got him to herself for a few minutes. 'There are things to say to you about Saturday night,' she said. 'I'd like a more private place than the middle of a busy A and E department, but this needs to be said quickly. I've been thinking about it quite a lot. In fact I've thought of little else.'

'Neither have I,' he said. 'Carly, I'm sorry if I caused you…'

Her voice was firm. 'Stop right there! You

didn't cause me anything. We did things together and I was a more than willing partner.'

'I am glad to hear that,' he said after a pause. 'Because I knew…when things had gone so far…I didn't want to stop.'

'I noticed,' she said with just a touch of a smile. 'And I felt the same way.'

'So where do we go now?' he asked.

'We go nowhere. Not at once. I know you've got problems, doubts, and so have I. Your life doesn't seem to be your own. I'm not sure what I want to do with mine. So we act as if we're just friends and colleagues. But we're not, are we, Alex?'

He was silent for a moment and then his voice was low as he said, 'No, Carly. You are far more to me than a friend. Though sometimes I wonder if things would have been easier if we'd stayed just friends.'

'Too late now,' she said with a grin. 'Alex, those words you spoke the other night—I can't get them out of my head. Even if I don't speak the language.'

'*Ya tebya lyublyu.* I love you,' he said slowly. 'I told you that. Perhaps I shouldn't have said it. I'm sorry…'

'Don't you dare say you're sorry! Tell me one thing. Did you mean it?'

'I did,' he said.

'It was one of the most wonderful things I have ever heard,' she told him.

It seemed to be the day for infectious diseases. Carly and Alex had just finished examining a baby, and had sent her up to the ward for overnight observation when Sister O'Brian appeared at the entrance to the cubicle.

'I can't be certain,' she said, 'but there's a child, a young boy, been brought in by his mother. He's very feverish and I think it's another infectious disease.'

'I'm sure you'll be right,' said Alex. 'What infectious disease do you think, Geraldine? Any idea?'

'Well, the family's just come back from Malaysia. They say that there's been quite a few cases of typhus fever there.'

'It's what?' Both Geraldine and Carly looked at Alex in alarm. Usually his voice was controlled; if he was angry or upset he spoke more quietly. But this had been almost a shout.

'Well, it's just a possibility,' Geraldine said nervously. Even the Sister had been shocked by Alex's outburst. 'But I could be wrong and I...'

'No, Geraldine, I am sure you're right. Let's go and see him at once.'

Another case that was very swiftly dealt with. Carly watched as Alex performed what seemed to be the quickest of examinations and then arranged for little Freddy to be admitted at once. He hardly spoke.

When the child was wheeled away they had a minute to sit down. Carly had the inevitable coffee but, when asked, Alex said he wanted nothing. He sat, leafing through an American medical magazine she had brought in. But Carly could tell that he was paying little attention to its contents.

He was still strangely silent now they had dispatched Freddy up to the paediatric ward, where special precautions were being taken to keep him from infecting the other children. Carly thought he was upset but as usual he managed to keep his emotions carefully hidden. What was different about this case?

'You know you're not to worry about Freddy,' she told him. 'We've caught him in plenty of time. Unless something goes seriously wrong, Freddy will be cured. We've got the drugs for him.'

He laughed, the most bitter sound she had ever heard. 'Yes, I know he'll be cured. It's easy if you have the right drugs. If they're available.'

She still couldn't understand what was wrong. 'Alex, tell me! Something's hurting you and I want to know what. Please tell me.'

It took a while but eventually he spoke. And what he said turned her world upside down again. 'The disease killed my wife. And my child.'

At first she was speechless, looked at him in horror. 'Your child? I knew you'd been married but I didn't know you had a child!'

'I don't have a child now. But I had a little girl,

aged four years. She was called Galina; it means bright one.'

His flat, matter-of-fact way of speech only made the horror worse for Carly. 'And she and your wife died of typhus fever? But it's curable; you're a doctor; there must have been some medicine available. It's doxycycline, isn't it? Couldn't you have…?'

'Evidently there was no doxycycline available.'

'Alex, please tell me more. You're being deliberately awkward. I didn't even know that you'd had a child; it would have made a difference to me and I…'

'They are dead now, gone. That is the end of it. There is no point in talking about it.'

'There is a point! You're hurting, it's obvious. If you share your pain, then it is lessened. And when you talk about them they are with you again. Sometimes it is a good thing to talk. Have you ever talked to anyone?'

'There's no one to talk to. I have no other family and I can deal with my pain alone.'

She was having difficulty in coping with this. 'You must feel so lonely. Alex, I can't push you but I really feel that you ought to say something Look, we mean something to each other. Lovers are supposed to share. Can't you just tell me how it was?'

When she looked at the icy bleakness of his face, she didn't need to be told. He was suffering still. Desperately, she wanted to ease his pain, to help him to come to terms with death, perhaps to start a new life. But if he wouldn't accept her help, there was nothing she could offer.

Then his face softened a little. He even managed a small smile. 'If I accepted help from anyone it would be from you,' he said. 'Perhaps, in time we might talk and…'

'We might talk? Alex, that's a promise. I'll hold you to it.'

'A promise?'

'Alex, two days ago we gave each other something. We both took, received. I want to give you something more. If I can.'

But now he was being guarded again. 'I'm not sure that I want to drag out things that…'

The door was pushed open and the SHO put her head round it. 'Just radioed in, RTA arriving, at least one badly injured child, possibly two.'

'Let's go to work,' Carly said, swallowing the rest of her coffee. Then, with some determination, 'Alex, this conversation isn't over. We'll finish it later.'

At last a small smile. 'You would fit in well with the people of Nyrova,' he said. 'You do not give up—whether there is hope or not.'

Was that a compliment? she wondered as they rushed down the corridor.

In fact their conversation was over for the day and the next few days. They found themselves working on two different cases; he was called to see John at the end of their shift and was away the next day. On the Saturday he was at a conference and on the Sunday she had arranged a day's leave. They were busy doctors; these things happened.

Of course she could have phoned him. But she

remembered what he had said about phone calls, how if you couldn't see the other person it was all too easy to get the wrong message. And she thought that their relationship was still a fragile one, that it would be all too easy to say the wrong thing without intending it. She needed to be face to face with him.

And so, early on Sunday afternoon, she drove over to the hospital to see him. She knew they couldn't have the conversation that she felt they needed. Almost certainly they'd be interrupted. In fact, it was entirely possible that he'd be busy, that there'd be no time at all for a conversation. But she could at least let him know that she was thinking of him.

In fact things must have been quiet because he came out to meet her. He had seen her parking her car from the window of the paediatric ward. She saw him walking across the tarmac to greet her and for some reason her heart gave an extra-special thump. He was gorgeous in his white coat!

She didn't get out of the car; she wasn't

staying long. She wound down her window and he came and leaned against the door.

'Carly, is everything all right, are you...?' Then he frowned as he saw how she was dressed. He looked in the car and saw the sheaf of lilies on the back seat.

'Black dress? Flowers? Is this a sad occasion?'

Was it a sad occasion? She wasn't quite sure herself, but she thought not. 'It's my mother's birthday,' she explained. 'She died not long ago. I'm meeting with my brothers and we're all going to put flowers on her grave. If we go together, well, it's not so sad an occasion. In a way it's joyous. When she died, I said at the funeral that this was to be a celebration of a life. And so that's what we try to do, to be happy as we celebrate her memory.'

He looked puzzled, curious. 'Celebrate?' he said. 'For me, I try to forget. Not bring them back.'

The expression in his dark eyes made her heart twist in sympathy. 'If you loved them then they don't go. Not entirely. Anyway, that's not why I came. Are you pleased to see me?'

'I am indeed. Over the past few days I have…
I have…' His voice trailed away.

She grinned at him. 'Go on,' she said. 'You'll
have to finish now. But I'll make it easier for
you. I came to see you just for five minutes
because I've missed seeing you. And now I've
seen you I feel happier. Now it's your turn.'

He looked at her wryly, shook his head. 'I
know no women like you,' he said. 'But you are,
of course, right. I have missed you. I am
enjoying my work here, I am making friends.
But the past few days have been hard without
you.'

'Good,' she said.

'But now you are here… I wish to catch a
memory.' He slipped his hand through the
window, clasped it lightly round her neck. Very
gently, he eased her head towards him. Then he
bent to the open window and kissed her.

An awkward position for a kiss, she thought.
Him bent double and her half leaning out of a car
window. But she closed her eyes and it was bliss.

Eventually he released her. 'I could get out of

the car,' she offered, disappointed that the kiss had stopped.

He shook his head. 'This was a tiny interlude, no more. But remembering it will keep me going through the rest of the day. Till tomorrow, Carly.'

He turned and strode back towards the hospital. He didn't look back at her, she noticed. She wondered if he ever looked back at anything.

Carly, Toby and Jack didn't stay long at the graveside, just enough time to lay their flowers. There was a few minutes' conversation, remembering who their mother had been and what she had done for them all. Then each said a short silent prayer and they turned to go back.

Toby had invited them back to his house for an early tea so they had a family meal, her two brothers and their two wives, three children and always the possibility of more. At first they talked a little about their mother. But they were determined not to be sad—they knew she wouldn't have wanted it. So they laughed and shouted and argued and it was—it was just fun.

Carly enjoyed it. As she sat, gently bouncing baby Esme on her knee, she thought of Alex—the man who was completely alone, who had no family and apparently didn't wish for one. She wondered if he had many friends—he seemed to have an abundance of acquaintances but there didn't seem to be anyone really close to him. His hospital was his life. That was good—but didn't he know what he was missing?

The children were put to bed, all in one room. Then Jack and Toby and their wives went out to dinner together. Carly had suggested this and said that she would babysit for the night. Her offer had been accepted with gratitude.

When they had gone Carly sat happily alone and thought of her day. It had been a good one. Now she could watch television, read or listen to CDs. But she decided to just sprawl on the couch and do nothing very much. It wasn't very often that she managed to do this. It felt vaguely, pleasantly decadent. So she poured herself a glass of the red wine that Toby had put out for her.

Her mother. Her mother had known she was dying, had accepted it calmly. Carly thought back to one of the last conversations they had had together. Her mother had told her how to live her life. 'You only get one chance, one life, so you have to make the most of it. I've tried to. Take risks if necessary. The worst thing I can think of is dying with your last thought being, If only I had…'

Carly had burst into tears, had asked her mother not to say any more. But now the words came back to her. Was she being too cautious, letting her past experiences affect her life? Was she ignoring her mother's advice?

What were her feelings for Alex? She was incredibly attracted to him. Every time she saw him, heard that deep voice, her body reacted to him. She thought that perhaps they could…perhaps he was the man for her. But she didn't know what he felt. He had said that he loved her, had said it in Russian. She had said it back to him. But so far they had gone no further than that. They had not had another meeting, although both knew that soon they would have to.

But she knew that she herself was being cautious. She was attracted to Alex—but she was still holding herself back. She had offered herself to him completely, had revelled in their togetherness. She blushed slightly as she thought of her behaviour on that occasion. She thought of the way in which she had abandoned all false modesty, had given herself to him as fully as she was able because she wanted to, needed to. She had given him everything. Never had she wondered if it was too much. Perhaps she ought to have done so.

She had committed herself before. She had thought that she had found the man with whom she could spend the rest of her life. And she had been betrayed. After that she thought she had learned her lesson. Don't get involved. And so far the only man she'd even been tempted to get involved with was Alex.

She laughed to herself, a little sadly. She knew

the nickname given to her brothers and herself.
The Good, the Bad and the Ugly. It was wrong,
of course. Jack wasn't ugly; Toby wasn't bad;
she certainly wasn't good. Now, when she
needed all her strength, she was just plain scared.

CHAPTER SEVEN

BUT it was good to be working with Alex next morning. If they were working together, Carly knew what the rules were. They were in A and E again, waiting for an ambulance to arrive, this time with children who had somehow been scalded at school. They stood just outside Reception, looking at the seats that were quickly being filled. Whenever possible, they avoided going into Reception itself. There was always someone who thought they could jump the queue, who would ignore the fact that they had been told that they would be called as quickly as possible. 'Are you a doctor? Well, I've been waiting for two hours now and I...'

It was always those who had nothing seriously wrong who approached them.

There was the rattle of feet behind them. Carly turned and tried to hide a smile when she saw who it was: Geraldine O'Brian. 'Alex, I've cleared a couple of cubicles for you. I'd like you to have Nurse Pelling with you in one— she's inexperienced and she needs someone a bit expert to show her how things should be done. And, since we're busy, I'll work the other one.'

'Efficient as ever, Geraldine,' Alex said. 'And that looks like the ambulance arriving now. Come on, you can give us a hand.'

It was weird. Carly thought that Alex and Sister Geraldine O'Brian were the oddest couple to be friends, but they were. Whenever it was possible for the two of them to work together, they did. When she asked Alex about it he told her that Sister O'Brian reminded him of his senior nurses in his home hospital. 'She knows her job. She goes out of her way to train other nurses. If there's an emergency, then she deals with it. And if anyone tries to stop her doing her job—then she deals with them too.'

The scalded children were quickly dealt with; happily there were none seriously hurt. And then Alex and Carly had the chance of a few moments together.

Yesterday he had kissed her, through the window of her car. Just over a week ago they had made love and it had been mind-shattering. They had said they loved each other. Now she was re-alising that they might be in love—but that in many ways they were still strangers. There was still much they had to tell each other, much to learn about each other. It might be hard.

They stood clutching mugs of tea in the doctors' room. 'How did your visit to your mother's grave go?' he asked after a moment.

'It went very well. I felt at one with her and my brothers, felt that she was with us. It made us all…well, regretful but also happy.'

'An unusual combination.' He seemed to think a little and then said, 'I envy you.'

'I would have invited you, but…well, you were working and it seemed to me an essentially family thing.'

'I agree with you entirely. Though now I feel that I would like to be a member of a family like yours. You said last week that we had been close to each other. And you weren't just talking about sex, you were talking about more than that. You are closer to me than anyone I know in this country—in any other country too.'

'I am?' His statement brought her so much pleasure. And also caused her some feeling of apprehension. 'Alex, what does it feel like to be suddenly closer to someone?'

'I would have said that very little frightens me. But being with you…it makes me feel so much alive. And I am frightened that it will all pass.'

'It doesn't have to,' she said. But she wondered if she was telling the truth.

'Anyway, we will just say that we are close. And I wish to presume on this closeness. Yesterday, after you left, I made some enquiries. There is a Russian Orthodox church in a suburb not too far from here. It was set up for Russian sailors in the early nineteenth century; apparently many of them settled here.'

'You belong to the Russian Orthodox Church?'

'If I belong to anything. Certainly my wife belonged. I phoned the priest, asked him some questions. I am going to visit the church on Wednesday afternoon. Not for a service, not to see anyone. Just to take some flowers. And I would like you to come with me.'

She stared at him, completely thrown by this request. 'You know I'd love to come with you,' she stammered in time. 'But why…what…?'

'I was thinking of you and your brothers. Of how you said you got peace, serenity, after you visited your mother's grave. I would like a similar peace myself.' Another of the small smiles that he occasionally permitted himself. 'Though I doubt I will ever be a serene man.'

'You could try a bit harder,' she suggested. 'It could happen.' He had come so far, she wondered if she could push him a little further. 'Alex, where is your family…where are your wife and daughter buried?'

'They are buried in a largely disused graveyard

about seventy miles from my hospital. There's a small Russian church, built of wood, and there are woods all around. Services are held there about once a month but not too many people attend.' He paused for a moment. 'I have never visited the grave since they died.'

She was horrified. 'Why not?'

He shrugged. 'I used to think that they had been alive and that now they were dead. The dead are no longer with us. But…talking to you has made me wonder if I was right.'

'Talking to me?' She was shocked.

'I told you, Carly, I feel closer to you than to anyone else I know.'

Carly wondered about this statement. She was so happy that Alex felt close to her. But she was realising that that closeness also brought respon-sibilities. Could she cope? She decided to move on to something safer, more mundane.

'Alex, if I go inside this church, what should I wear?'

'Possibly things are more relaxed here, I just don't know. But in Nyrova you would wear some kind of covering for your head. And perhaps a skirt rather than trousers.'

'I think I can manage that,' she said.

It wasn't too hard for her to get Wednesday after-noon off. He picked her up and they set off for the Russian Orthodox Church. 'Why exactly do you want me to go to this church with you?' she asked after a while. 'How do you think I will help?'

As so often with him, there was a long pause before he answered. Then, 'You are having an effect on me. More than anyone…anyone since my wife died. I pay attention to you. I also have told you that I love you. I have said that to no one since Irina's death. Perhaps this is a way of telling her what I feel about you.'

He seemed surprised at saying this, as if it was a new idea. Carly was surprised too, and a bit ap-prehensive. She had always felt that whatever re-lationship she started with Alex, then she would be able to deal with the consequences. Now she was not so sure. 'So how have I had this effect on you?'

'I noticed that when you talked about visiting your mother's grave, you talked about her happily. And that the next day, after you had returned from the visit, you seemed…even happier? I have always kept my grief to myself. I have never talked to anyone about my wife and child. I thought that in time the pain would go. But it didn't…it hasn't. So this is a bit of an experiment. I just want to see how things go. And I want you with me because…'

She interrupted him, stumbling over the words, but she knew he knew what she meant. 'Because *ya tebya lyublyu.*'

'Because I love you,' he agreed.

When they got there Carly decided not to go into the church. She told Alex that she would wait outside, that this was a visit he should make by himself. In a sense he was saying a goodbye, and she didn't know the people he was saying goodbye to.

He thought about this for a moment, then nodded. 'I think you are right.' Carrying his flowers, he went silently into the church.

Twenty minutes later he came out. His face, as so often, was unreadable. 'All right, Alex?' she asked, knowing that the question was foolish but unable to think of anything else to say.

Surprisingly, he took the question seriously, thought about it. 'I am glad that I came,' he said. 'Shall we drive back?'

Their route back to the hospital took them along the tree-lined river bank. On the grey water they could see oil-tankers slowly moving downstream; on the far bank houses appeared like toys. 'Alex, pull in here,' she said after a while. 'I just want to sit and talk to you and I want to be able to see your face.'

He didn't question her request but drove down away from the traffic and parked in a sheltered spot where they faced the promenade.

'You have questions for me,' he said. It was more a statement than a query.

'I need to get to know you. You're a secretive man—but there are no secrets between lovers.'

'That is true.' He took her hand, held it

between his two. 'It may be hard for me but I will answer as best I can.'

The first question had to be brutal. 'How long since your wife and child died?' she asked.

'Five years.'

The next question was delicate. 'Has…has there been no other woman in your life since then?'

Now he grinned. 'Why do you want to know?'

She blushed slightly. 'Because I think you are…you are too much of a man to remain celibate for all that time.'

'I have my work and I am dedicated to it. But there have been a couple of affairs. They were short, a case of giving and taking some small comfort. No one was hurt. I made it clear from the start that whatever we had could only be temporary.'

Carly felt jealous. And she wondered how the women had felt when they were told so clearly that the affair would only be temporary. 'Did you ever think you might love one of them?' she asked, though dreading the answer. 'Did they love you?'

His answer was hard. 'Perhaps one did love

me. She was upset when I said things had to end. But there was no way that I could pretend something was there when it was not.'

He turned his head, glanced at her curiously. 'Why are you so interested, Carly?'

She didn't want to think about this herself. She thought she might not like her own answer. 'Just curious,' she said.

His next question stunned her. 'Are you thinking about you and me? If you might be another woman with whom I had a short and pointless relationship?'

'That's not fair!' she gasped eventually. 'I don't think that at all.'

Remorselessly he went on, 'I want to be fair. I want to tell you—whatever happens—that you mean more to me than anyone since…since…'

'You don't have to say it,' she said, covering his hand with hers. 'I know since when.'

'Carly Sinclair, you're getting to know me too well,' he growled.

'And the more I get to know you, the better I like you. And that's different from loving you.'

There was a comfortable silence for a few minutes and then she said, 'I've never seen your flat.'

'There's little to see. I'm not like you, a home-maker. There are no pictures, no flowers; I am happier when things are plain. My flat is just a place to eat, sleep and store my clothes.'

'I'd still like to see it,' she said firmly. 'Why don't you cook tea for me?'

'We could go out for dinner; I'd like that.'

'Well, I wouldn't. I want to eat with you in your flat.'

He laughed. 'I can order something in, perhaps.'

'And wine with the meal?'

'I have a couple of bottles in. Why exactly do you want to come, Carly?'

'I think I'll know you better if I see you in your room. You can tell a lot about a person from the place where they live. I've just told you, in many ways I still don't know you. And I want to know you.'

'An English evening,' he said. 'A takeaway meal. And we can watch television if we wish.'

His flat was as plain as he had said. Clean, of course, but completely without personality. 'Not one single picture?' she asked, gazing round. 'No photographs, no ornaments?'

Alex was amused at her reaction. 'There are no pictures, ornaments, because I don't live here,' he said. 'I just exist. This is not my home.'

He had picked the wrong word and she seized on it. 'You don't want a home,' she said, 'and I'll bet where you live in Russia is just like this. You're scared of having a home.'

For a moment she thought she had gone too far. His face went blank, icy cold. Then he nodded and said, 'You are very perceptive, Carly. Perhaps that is true.'

She didn't want to go into this, decided to back off. 'I'm hungry,' she said. 'What can we have to eat?'

He took a sheaf of menus from the local fast-food shops and handed them to her. 'Anything from any one of these,' he said. 'But now you've seen the place, are you sure we can't go to a restaurant? Dine out with just a touch of style?'

'No. We eat in here, have a domestic evening and perhaps we can talk.'

'Talk?' he asked and she blushed.

Carly felt that they both knew that there was a conversation to be finished. But they seemed to agree that it could wait a while. They ordered a Chinese banquet and it was delivered promptly. They made polite small talk over the meal, drank some wine and often were companionably silent. Then they sat side by side on his couch over coffee—and it was the time to talk.

She was nervous. There were things she needed to know about him, but she wasn't sure how the knowledge would affect her.

'I need to know more about your wife and child,' she said. 'You promised you would tell me.'

Alex looked at her steadily for a while and then went to his bedroom. It was quite some time before he returned, carrying an envelope that looked to contain some documents or pictures.

'It took you long enough to find,' she said.

'It was buried under some luggage, I wasn't quite sure where. I don't look at these very often.'

'But you do look at them sometimes?'

'Yes. Occasionally.' A curt answer. She recognised now that it was not ill manners—it was just that he had little to say and saw no reason to explain the fact.

'I have told you a little about the place where I work, the people I work with. That is the background you must remember when I tell you of my marriage. Without that knowledge, this story is…is stupid.'

'One thing you have never been, Alex, is stupid. I know that, you know it. Now tell me about Irina.'

He looked at her for a while and she knew he was still debating quite what to tell her. She could feel his indecision and she knew he hated not being able to make up his mind. And she could also feel his pain. But then he seemed to make up his mind. 'Very well.' But he still paused before opening the envelope and shaking out photographs. Not many, perhaps five or six.

He selected one. 'This is a picture of Irina and myself on our wedding day.'

Carly peered intently at the picture. Alex first. Instantly she recognised the tall muscular body; it didn't seem to have changed. There were fewer lines on his face and he was smiling. He was smiling down at his bride with an expression of love that made Carly feel instantly envious. No one had ever looked at her like that. But she recognised the expression; she had seen it on the faces of her brothers and their wives. It was more than an expression of love. There was happiness, a realisation that love had just been celebrated, made permanent. Then she felt angry at herself for being envious.

She turned to Irina, who was beautiful. But she was nothing like Carly, in face, figure or hair. Irina was blonde; Carly's hair was dark. Irina's face was a perfect oval; Carly's was more pointed. Irina was slim to the point of thinness; Carly was…well, womanly.

'She's very beautiful,' Carly said honestly. 'Her hair is beautiful.'

'A few of the local people are blonde. They believe that they are the descendants of the armies of Alexander the Great. Possibly it is true.'

He flicked over the rest of the photographs. 'The other four are pictures of my daughter as she grew up.'

Perhaps he didn't want to talk about each individual picture. Perhaps it was too painful. But as Carly glanced up at his face there was no obvious pain. Just the shuttered expression she had seen so often before.

Galina had been a beautiful baby—just like her mother—or her father. Her mother held her in one photograph, her father in the other three. Carly was fascinated as she stared at picture after picture, seeing the transition from baby to child, seeing the evidence of growing intelligence. When Galina was four, Carly thought she could see a resemblance to her father; she had that earnest, questioning look that children of that age often developed. What must it be like to have lost a child like this? Carly felt tears in her eyes. But she had to remain detached.

She looked at the pictures again and something struck her. Alex was in four of the pictures. Obviously Irina had been the photographer in the family. But it was a different Alex from the one she knew.

'Alex, you used to smile an awful lot more.' Then she silently cursed herself for her insensitivity.

But he didn't seem to be too worried. 'Perhaps I had more to smile about,' he said.

There was still more she needed to know. 'So tell me what happened,' she asked gently.

His reply was quiet, calm. 'You've seen pictures of the area; you know how it is miles from anywhere. It's not very productive; the weather can be dreadful and life is harsh. But the people learn to accept it. They are tough, resilient.'

He leaned back by her side, his unfocused gaze on the opposite wall. As he spoke, Carly realised that he was talking as much to himself as to her.

He was reflecting on his life, perhaps wondering how things might change—if he wanted them to.

'You know my ancestors came from the area but I never lived there as a child. I heard about it, wondered about it. I determined that one day I would go there. We lived in Moscow—my parents died in a car crash when I was nineteen, so I was never encouraged by them to visit. And then I was too busy getting on in the medical world even to think about the place. I don't think I had a holiday in over eight years.

'Then I got offered a job—a one-year placement in New York; it would have been a great opportunity, working with some of the best physicians in the world. I said I'd go. But the job didn't start for three months. And so, I thought, why not take a short break? I'll see where my family came from. I made a few enquiries, found there was a hospital there, wrote, sent my CV and asked if they'd like a doctor for three months—for free.'

He laughed, though there was as much sadness as humour in the sound.

'I didn't get a reply. So, with much trouble, I managed to phone the hospital director. He said he'd received my letter but hadn't replied because he thought it was rather a cruel joke. What doctor with my qualifications would want to come to the back of beyond that was Nyrova? When I persuaded him that it was not a joke, he was overwhelmed. And said they'd be delighted to offer me a post.'

Another laugh. 'It seemed a change from the hospital conditions in New York.'

'But you went?'

'Oh, yes, nothing could stop me now. I was motivated by a combination of curiosity and awkwardness.'

'Why awkwardness?'

'Everyone was telling me that this was the back of beyond, the medicine was paltry, the people unpredictable, the weather dreadful. So I went.'

'Did you enjoy it?'

He shrugged. 'It was a culture shock. A kind of medicine that I had never seen before. Making do with ancient equipment, managing without a regular drug supply, dealing with suppliers that never seemed to get anything right. But I liked the people. And then I met Irina; she was a nurse there. She was gorgeous.'

'I can see that from her photograph,' Carly said, feeling a slight twinge of pain.

'Well, I fell in love with her. I didn't expect to; I didn't intend to. For a start, I didn't have time for a relationship. Then I found that she was more than gorgeous; she was tough. She didn't want anything to do with me.'

He smiled at the memories. 'It was hard. I thought she might get to like me but she said she was not going to be the plaything of a man who would disappear out of her life after three months. I asked her out a dozen times; each time she said no. Then, for some reason, I had to call at her home. She lived with her mother and father and her great-grandmother—a super old lady who was ninety-five.'

'And?'

'It was unbelievable. The old lady had actually worked in my family home as a maid; she re-

membered my great-grandparents. She told Irina
that any Braikovitch was a good man. My great-
grandfather had been a kind landlord, had looked
after his tenants. She was sure his great-grandson
would be a good doctor and a good man. So
Irina went out with me. Not that there was
anywhere much to go to. One month, two
months, two and a half months. I asked Irina to
marry me; she said that she loved me, that she
wanted to—but she could not leave her home
town. She just couldn't; she'd never be happy
anywhere else. And she could not ask me to give
up my career. We had to part.'

'Tough is the right word to describe her,'
Carly muttered.

'So we negotiated. We would get married, I
would give up my place in America, stay on in
Nyrova for three years. Then she would come
with me wherever I wanted to go.'

Carly was spellbound. 'Let's get this straight.
You gave up your career—for love? Alex, I'd
never have thought it of you, but you're a
romantic. A true one.'

His smile was bitter. 'A romantic? Me? See where romance got me. I was married, I was happy at home and happy at my work. After a year we had a little girl and I doted on her. There was no more talk of my leaving, although I did sometimes miss high level medicine.'

'So what happened then?' Carly felt that she now knew so much more about Alex. He had told her things about himself that opened up an entire new perspective—this was a man she didn't know. But a man she very much wanted to know. Where was the harsh, unsentimental doctor now?

Then she realised. This was only half the story.

'What happened then?' He repeated her words slowly.

'There was an epidemic. An outbreak of typhus fever. Just a minor local epidemic, but of a particularly virulent strain. And it was decimating the local population. Epidemics like this aren't uncommon out there, you know. Especially in the hot summer months. Work in the hospital was non-stop; I was regularly turning in an eighteen-hour day. Irina was pregnant again. I wanted her to leave the town but she insisted that she stay. The hospital was badly short of staff and she was needed.

'But I sent Galina, our daughter, to a remote village about seventy miles away. There wasn't even a telephone there. Irina's parents went with her. The epidemic hadn't reached the village; she would be safe.'

There was a change in quality in his voice. At first it seemed that it was as controlled as ever, but Carly thought she could detect a thickening in his tone. She had the impression that he was making a vast mental effort to remain calm, detached, to talk about this as if it was just another medical emergency. But it was not.

'You know the treatment for typhoid fever is simple?' he went on. 'One single oral dose of doxycycline should provide a cure. But I didn't have enough drugs for my needs; it was in very short supply. I kept on demanding more from my suppliers but there was never enough. People were dying from the lack of it.'

A long pause now, the longest yet. She put her hand over his, tried to reassure him. 'It does help, to talk,' she said. 'You can't stop now. The worst will soon be over; there's not much more to tell, is there? Please go on, Alex. You will feel better for sharing.'

'Irina and I worked at the hospital until the disease was in recession. Fewer and fewer cases were being reported; I thought we'd got it beaten. Then Irina contracted the disease; she was practically the last case. She was pregnant, she was run-down, the supply of doxycycline had ended. And she died.' He paused, took a breath. 'Then I went to see my daughter and found only one member of the family alive— Irina's father—and he died the day after. I had been wrong; the disease had reached the village. My wife, my child, my unborn child, my adopted family, all dead. Galina had already been buried. I arranged for Irina to be buried next to her.'

Carly tried to imagine the enormity of this horror, and failed. 'So what did you do?'

'Irina talked to me before she died. She said she loved me. She said Galina loved me. She said if I loved both of them I would work at the hospital until the epidemic was over. And then I could leave. But now I knew I wouldn't leave. There was nothing for me anywhere in the world. All I had wanted had been taken from me. And this was the land of my forefathers; I owed it to them to stay. I liked the people; my wife and child had died here. And I had fallen in love with the land, harsh and unwelcoming though it was. I stayed.'

Carly could feel the tears now running down her cheeks, knew she was sobbing and that there was nothing she could do about it. Alex wrapped his arm round her shoulders, hugged her gently. 'Don't take on so much,' he said. 'It's over now and it's a long time ago. I'm sorry I told you, upset you.'

'Oh, Alex,' she choked. 'Alex, you've suffered so, so much.'

She had asked him to explain things to her, had thought perhaps she could help him. And now he was comforting her. She loved him for it.

He left his arm round her for the next ten minutes. Then he stood and fetched two glasses. 'Brandy,' he said, offering her one. 'Take it; you will feel better.'

She didn't believe him, but she sipped the fiery spirit and after another ten minutes she did indeed feel strong again. Well, stronger. She had said that talking about things would help. Perhaps they still could. 'So how do you feel about them now?' she asked.

'Partly I feel guilty. I was a doctor and I was a family man. I had a dual responsibility. I had sacrificed one responsibility; I should have taken better care of my family.'

'You did what you felt was best under such awful circumstances,' Carly suggested gently. 'You couldn't have done more. Alex, you'll never forget your family, but maybe it's time you allowed yourself to move on from the past.'

He shook his head. 'The past is always with us and the pain is always with me. But I can live with it. Just one thing. I will never suffer like that again. And I will never let anyone suffer as I did.'

Carly's brow creased; she thought about this for a moment. 'You won't let anyone suffer?' she quoted him. 'You mean me, don't you? Alex, are you trying to warn me off you?'

'Yes, Carly. I do love you and I know you love me. But I have seen too much, you have seen too little. Life for you is still sweet, will always be so.'

Carly looked at him. 'Certainly no one I have loved—well, loved like you did—has died. But don't be so sure that life has always been sweet for me too.'

'You have suffered?'

Well, yes, she had. And it had hurt. But not like him. 'I have suffered. However, as I said, no one died.' But the pain had felt like dying.

Gently he said, 'But I am sure there was still pain. At times you show it.'

He glanced at his watch. 'Carly, for me, for you, this has been a…momentous afternoon and evening. There are things to be thought about. But perhaps now I should take you home.'

'No, I'm going to stay. I don't know if I need you or you need me most. But we do need to be together.' There was a pause. He said nothing, so she went on, 'Don't you want me, Alex?'

He pulled her to him and kissed her, passionately, desperately. 'Of course I want you. I've never wanted anything more. The past five years has been a time in darkness, now you have brought me light. You mean more to me than…'

'Too much talking,' she whispered softly. 'Just take me to bed and hold me.'

CHAPTER EIGHT

WORKING together the next day was odd, and curiously exciting. She and Alex were different from the couple they had been before. They were bonded more.

As ever, they were busy. Sometimes they had to confer on a patient but mostly they passed each other in the corridor with a brief smile and an occasional word. She would lean towards him as they passed, brush her hand against his arm. And he would smile again.

What was different was that now she thought that she knew him. He was no longer an enigma to her; he was a man with troubles and a history and she thought she understood him. He had given her something of himself.

Only later in the afternoon did she remember that gifts often brought responsibilities.

They worked late that day and then he had to go for a meeting with members of MedAsia. She would have to spend the evening without seeing him. Well, it had happened often enough before; they were both busy doctors. But she would have liked to have seen him. She decided not to go home straight away but had a meal in the canteen and then went to do some slightly neglected studying in the hospital library.

An evening alone in her flat. Once—not so long ago—she would have looked forward to it. Tonight she seemed less than keen. She had a bath, put on her dressing gown and made herself a hot milky drink. Then she wandered around her flat, picking a favourite CD to play, gazing at the photographs on the wall. She looked at her bookcase, ignored the heavy medical tomes and for a moment glanced through a much-loved, much-read book she had been given as a school prize many years ago. *Famous Female*

Explorers. It gave accounts of a handful of women travellers in the nineteenth and early twentieth century who had made extraordinary trips to some of the world's still unexplored regions. 'These courageous women', it called them in the preface. She sighed and shut the book with a snap. She wasn't feeling courageous.

But it was good to be at home, alone, in her own perfectly organised flat. Here she was always safe, comfortable, at peace. Then for a moment she wondered. What kind of ambition was it for a young professional woman to want nothing but to be safe, comfortable and at peace? Was there to be no striving, no excitement in her life?

So she sat on her couch and thought of Alex.

She had learned so much more about him; his behaviour had become so much more understandable. Now she could sympathise with the barrier he put up against the world and his apparent coldness. It was his defence.

Then something else struck her. It was the last

thing people would think of Alex, but now she knew him better than most. Beneath that hard exterior, he was vulnerable. Even if he didn't understand it himself, what he had told her was a cry for help.

Could she help him—was she strong enough? Once again she thought of her mother's advice—always to go for what you really wanted.

The next thought was the most provoking of all. Of course she was concerned about Alex; she did want him to be happy. But she didn't want to be his counsellor. She wanted them to be in love.

Well, they were in love. Just the sight of him in the distance now made her shiver with excitement and desire. But there was more to think about than that. That was now. What about the future? It struck her that Alex had never mentioned what was going to happen to them. Like her, he seemed to want to exist solely in the present. But there was a future. What would it bring them?

Enough dreaming. She had been asked for

some details of the work on microsurgery that she had been doing in Chicago; time to look it out for the next day. She went to pull out a dusty trunk from the wardrobe in her spare bedroom, sorted through piles of notes, letters, old mementoes of her time in America. She found the microsurgery details quite quickly. But then there was some stuff to throw away, other stuff to smile over and remember.

It came as a shock. She flipped open a folder and there he was, smiling at her. A large photograph of Dennis Clarkson, as handsome and debonair as ever, eyes twinkling at the camera as they used to twinkle at her.

Just for a second she stared at his face, remembering what he had done to her. Slowly, deliberately, she picked up the picture, tore it in half, in half again and then into as many tiny pieces as possible. As she did so she saw the inscription written boldly across the bottom of the photograph. *For my darling Carly, yours forever. All my love, Dennis.*

There were bits of torn paper all over the floor.

That would teach her to get irate; she'd now have to pick them all up. And, as she did so, after a while she found herself smiling. Dennis had been an episode out of her past. He was gone. She realised that he was behind her; never again would his memory trouble her. She could even forget his deceit and remember the odd good time they had had together. He was a weak character; she had known that but had tried to ignore it. Now she had met someone who was strong. And the difference was obvious.

She went to bed and slept soundly. And her dreams were of Alex.

She had plans when she went to work the next morning. She would invite Alex back to her flat that evening for a meal, cook for him. And if he wanted to stay the night—then he'd be most welcome. When she thought about the easy way she had just decided this, her cheeks warmed a little. This was a vastly different Carly from the woman she had been only a month before. Then she decided she liked being the new her.

Alex was delighted with her invitation. 'Just one thing,' he said. 'I buy the wine. In fact, let's go and buy it together. There's rather a good wine shop I've been told about that's not too far away. Then I'll sit and drink wine while you fuss around in the kitchen and prepare the evening meal.'

'Alex! There are some things you don't even joke about!'

'Sorry,' he said with a grin. 'I'll offer to peel the potatoes.'

'You can sit just outside the kitchen and tell me more about your work in your hospital. I want to know everything about you and it.'

So, when work was finished, they set off for the wine shop in Alex's car. They were driving down a dual carriageway when a black car overtook them at a frightening speed. It shot past, engine screaming, then swerved in front of them with a squeal of tyres. Alex had to slam his foot on the brake. 'What the…?' he started to say.

From the car in front appeared an arm; a quick upraised finger signalled defiance and then the car lurched forward, accelerating towards the bend at the end of the road.

Carly sighed and tried to calm her quickly beating heart. 'The driver was only a kid,' she said, shaking her head.

'What should we do? They're going to cause an accident and…'

'We can't do anything and hopefully the police will be on to them by now. Let them deal with it; they're professionals. It isn't our business.'

'They could have crashed into us. I'd like to deal with them myself.'

'I sympathise, Alex. But just try to live with it.'

Still moving at a lunatic pace, the black car disappeared round the bend ahead. And then they both heard the screech of tyres. And then the noise of rending metal.

'I think it might just have become our business,' Alex said.

The bend at the end of the road was a sharp one. The black car had taken it too fast and the driver had lost control. The car had rolled, skidded on its side and smashed into a wall.

There was something pathetic about the filthy underside of it, the still rolling wheels.

Carly had taken her mobile out, was already dialling 999. Alex stopped some distance from the crashed car. He got out and approached it cautiously. When she had relayed her message, emphasised its urgency, Carly followed him.

They both went to the front of the car, peered through the shattered windscreen. Carefully, Alex kicked the shattered glass aside. There were three youths there. Fortunately, the two in the front had put on their safety belts. They looked dazed, cut by flying glass. But the one in the back had been thrown to one side when the car had rolled; he lay there, unconscious.

'Alex, I'll take the unconscious one, you check the other two. The paramedics will be here in a moment. Let's just make sure everyone can breathe, no one is actually bleeding to death and they can't injure themselves any further.'

Luckily, the unconscious lad was breathing and had a strong pulse, so the two doctors just monitored the three casualties until they heard the siren of the ambulance.

The paramedics were good. One man, one woman, they introduced themselves as Harry and Angela. They listened to Alex's report as they made their own initial assessment and then Angela said, 'Thanks for your help. We'll take over, but we might need you again if you wouldn't mind waiting around?'

So they stood back and watched. The youth in the back had been strapped into a stretcher, his entire body immobilised until he could be X-rayed. But the only way he could be taken out of the car was by the back door, which had been forced open and pointed to the sky. Angela called to Alex for some help, so he climbed on to the side of the car and helped Harry ease the stretcher upwards and then pass it to Angela on the ground.

It was quickly done. And then, just as Alex was about to jump down from the side of the car, it rocked. The opened door quivered, slammed downwards. And on its downward path it smashed into Alex's ribs.

Carly winced as she heard his grunt of pain. Winced again as he half toppled, half jumped to the ground.

Angela turned at once. 'You're hurt; let me see.'

'No problem, just a bruise. Honestly, Angela, there's nothing to worry about, see to this three here.'

The paramedic shook her head. 'I can't leave possibly injured people at the scene of a crash.'

'I'm a doctor, my friend here is a doctor. This is not serious, believe me. She will look after me if I need it. And I live in the grounds of Dell Owen; we'll drive to A and E ourselves.'

'Well, if you're going to do that, then…'

'I'll see he's all right,' said Carly. And it was decided.

They made their way to his car. 'I'm driving,' said Carly. 'There's no argument. Your face is pale, your hands are shaking, your breathing is rapid. You're going into shock. I'll have you in A and E in…'

'No! I want no fuss. You can patch me up if I need any patching up. I've been invited to tea at

your flat; that's where I want to go.' Somehow
he managed a smile.

She hesitated a minute. Then, 'Okay, my flat.
But you accept that I'm the doctor and if I want
you in A and E, then you go.'

'Agreed,' he said after a minute. 'Now, can we
start, please?'

She was a doctor. For the moment Alex was her
patient, not her lover; she had to be detached.
But it was hard. She could feel his pain, wanted
to comfort him, wanted to wrap her arms round
him and… She was a doctor!

She dealt with the possible shock first, giving
him tea with sugar in it—which he detested—
and making sure that he was warm and comfortable. Then she took a close look at the injury. She
might have guessed. It was more serious than he
had admitted.

He lay on her bed, dressed simply in dark blue
boxers. In spite of the dressing he was holding
to his side, blood trickled on to the towel she had
stretched underneath him.

The sharp corner of the door had ripped a five-inch gash along the line of his ribs. Carefully, Carly felt the bones, here so near to the skin. 'Does it hurt when you breathe? Take a deep breath—but do it slowly.'

Of course, he knew what she was doing. 'No deep pain. There may be bruising but I'm pretty sure that nothing is broken.'

She felt anyway, noticing that he didn't flinch, even when she must have been causing him pain. 'I think you're right. And, after I've cleaned it up, I think I can hold the cut together with butterfly stitches. But you're going to have to move very carefully for the next few days. Bending, turning only carefully, above all no picking up weights.'

'No, Doctor,' he said ironically.

'We'll get started, then.'

She tried one last time to persuade him to go to A and E, but he refused. 'I could deal with this easily, so can you. Going to A and E would only cause fuss and confusion. And if you think you haven't got enough bandages and so on here, there's a very full medical kit locked in the boot of my car.'

She was curious about this. 'Why do you carry that with you?'

'Habit. I always carry a kit in Nyrova. You never know when there's going to be an emergency. And the chances are that you might be miles from help.'

'I see.'

In fact, not much medical skill was needed. Half an hour and she had finished. Gingerly, he climbed off her bed and felt what movements he could make without causing himself pain. 'I could do with a bath,' he said, 'but I guess I'll have to make do with a wash. And have you a dressing gown or something I could borrow? I don't really want to get back into these bloody clothes.'

'Nothing that'll fit you. I'll get you a couple of towels. Now, are you hungry?'

An expression of surprise crossed his face. 'You know, I am. I'd forgotten I was being invited to tea.'

'Well, I'm not cooking now. I'll phone for a

meal. I'll make you another drink of tea and then you can go for your wash. You'll feel better afterwards.'

'Carly, I'm all right, you know.'

'Just for the moment I'm the doctor, not you. How would you treat a man who came into A and E with that gash? Honest answer, Alex.' She smiled at his reluctant expression.

'Okay, you win. I'd probably keep him in for a while. Just for observation.'

'Right. Have a wash and then we'll eat. Then you stay the night here. I'm not having you on your own.'

'Here? With you?'

'In my bed. And I sleep on my couch.'

'But Carly, I couldn't…'

'I'm your doctor now. You can and you will.' Then she grinned and said, 'I just don't have a dressing gown your size. But you can wrap a couple of my big towels round yourself.'

'As you wish.' After he had drunk his tea, he went to her bathroom. She phoned the order for the meal and set out the little dining table. Wine might not be a good idea; they could drink fruit juice or water.

'I feel a fool like this. But I'm not going to sit around in just my underwear.'

Carly turned and blinked at the apparition before her. A white towel was wrapped round his waist. Another towel was draped shawl-like over his shoulders. She could see his broad chest, the sprinkling of hair across it, the muscles curving on shoulders and upper arms. For a moment her body reacted to his; she felt his essential maleness, wanted to... The doorbell rang.

'That'll be the food,' she gabbled. 'Alex, sit down at the table.' She fled downstairs.

After the meal she felt better. She thought he felt the same; there was more colour in his cheeks and a more thoughtful look in his eyes. And she was constantly aware of his nakedness under the towels, catching glimpses of muscles, of taut skin. They sat side by side on the couch and she wondered how their evening would progress. But for the moment they could chat.

'You say that in Nyrova you always carry an

extensive medical kit in your car,' she said. 'How often does it get used?'

'Often enough for it to be a good idea. But out there I carry even more. I even carry a portable anaesthetic kit. I once had to perform an emergency Caesarean.'

'What? On your own?'

'I was in a tiny village, miles from anywhere, certainly miles from my hospital. I'd been checking on an outbreak of flu; I just wanted to be quite sure it wasn't anything more serious. In fact it wasn't. But, as I was leaving, the local midwife came to see me. A lot of the births in my area are dealt with very adequately by the local midwives. They don't have much training; many of them got their skills from their mothers. But they do a good enough job. Unfortunately, this was a job she couldn't manage.'

'A pregnant woman needed a Caesarean?'

'Exactly. She needed it urgently. There I was, miles from my hospital, miles from the nearest theatre, without a single trained doctor, anaesthetist or nurse to assist me. Just a fifty-year-old midwife who was delivering babies using the same techniques as had been used for the past two hundred years.'

'So what did you do?' Carly was both fascinated and appalled.

'I got the women in the household to scrub out a room. Everything—walls ceiling, floor. Then they scrubbed the kitchen table. And the midwife and I performed a Caesarean. It was the first time she'd ever seen such a thing. I had to tell her what to do, what to hold, where to put her fingers, where to hold flesh back. And she did it, though I could tell that she was terrified. She'd never seen, done, anything like that before. But she did it and I couldn't have managed without her.'

'And?'

'We succeeded. Mother and child did well. The midwife asked me if I'd get her the kit I'd used, give her a few lessons. I had to say no.'

Carly shivered. 'Must be a different kind of medicine out there.'

'It is. But remember, medicine is ultimately about doctors and nurses as well as drugs and instruments. If you have the skill and the knowledge you can do an awful lot of good.'

'I'll believe you. Thousands wouldn't.'

He stretched an arm behind her head, eased her towards him and kissed her. Kissed her on the lips. A gentle kiss. The kiss of a lover. And after a millisecond she responded.

She felt happy there, felt all of her senses responding to him. Tiny things seemed important, more obvious than they should be. There was the dressing she had taped on his chest, the pure white of the lint contrasting with the darker skin. There was the smell—her expensive soap mixed excitingly with the warmth of his body. There was the taste of his lips, his tongue—even a faint memory of the cranberry juice they had been drinking. And touch. The roughness of the towel, the softness of his skin. This was Alex. Her Alex. But was he her Alex? Would he ever truly be hers?

He leaned back but left his hand behind her head, stroking, caressing the back of her neck.

Softly, he said, 'Just for the tiniest moment there, when I kissed you, you hesitated.'

He had noticed! She hadn't known he was so perceptive. 'Well, a first kiss—it's always a bit of a
surprise.' She tried to make little of what he had
felt.

He was not to be fooled. 'It wasn't our first
kiss, Carly. Every time I kiss you there is that
first anxiety. You told me once that you too had
suffered, that life had not been all sweet to you.'

'Why don't you kiss me again and just stop
talking?' It was a suggestion of semi-desperation.
She didn't think she wanted this conversation.

She should have remembered how tenacious
he could be. 'I dearly want to kiss you again. But
you persuaded me to tell you my story, persuaded me that afterwards I would—I could—feel
better for it. I didn't believe you but I was wrong
and talking to you did indeed lessen the pain.'

To her surprise he kissed her again, this time
a quick brushing of the lips. She liked it, she
wanted more, she tried to pull him back to her.
But he resisted. 'No, Carly. Well, not yet. Now
you have to tell me what went wrong, what
ruined your life. Just as I told you.'

'Nothing ruined my life; you're imagining things! My brothers and me, we're the Good, the Bad and the Ugly! I'm the Good; my life is perfect.'

'No, it is not. Tell me, Carly.' This time he did not kiss her. Instead he took her hands in his, held them against his naked chest. She could feel the warmth, the powerful heartbeat. And, mysteriously, it gave her strength.

'All right,' she said, 'I'll tell you. But you're to keep hold of my hands.'

'I will do that.'

'It's not a tragic story like yours. It's just a mean, ordinary story about a mean, ordinary man.'

'I was loved to the end,' he said. 'I keep that memory within me and it gives me strength. You, I suspect, were betrayed. You have nothing to look back on but deceit. The thing to do is not to look back.'

She knew he was trying to give her strength. And he was succeeding, she could tell him. She took a breath and started.

'I went to work in the Chicago Dana Hospital for six months. With Professor Larry Laker; he was doing some pioneering work on micro-surgery. A brilliant man—I learned a lot from him. The work was hard but I had a good salary and so I took on a great little flat. More than I could really afford, but it was worth it for the pool and the gym alone. What I didn't have was friends. Not yet. And I was…well, I'd worked hard all through my medical career so far. I hadn't bothered with much of a social life. I'm supposed to be the good one of the three of us. A better word might have been innocent. Or in-experienced. Or just plain stupid.'

'Carly! Don't put yourself down! Everyone makes mistakes; the test is if you learn from them. And you did!'

'Did I?' she asked bitterly. 'Well, perhaps. I think I learned to distrust every man I met after that.' He was holding her hands lightly in his lap. She gripped his hands, squeezed them.

'Just a common story. Dr Dennis Clarkson. About ten years older than me, working his way up the medical ladder, specialising in plastic surgery. A good earner that, in America. We met at a get-together party the week I flew out there. He was gorgeous! Blond curly hair, bronzed, the physique that comes from playing a lot of tennis. And well-dressed. Always well-dressed. He spent more on clothes in a month than I did in a year. And his car? Well, just guess.'

Alex nodded. 'Sports car, open top. Probably red, probably from abroad rather than America.'

'Nearly perfect. A silver Porsche. He took me home from the party in it, I invited him in for a coffee and then we…' She swallowed. 'Well, he stayed the night. I cooked him breakfast and I thought that that would be it. Why should he bother with anyone like me? But he did. He took me to dinner that night. And two nights after that. And then we went away for a weekend together; it was magic.

'Every day seemed better. After a while he suggested that he might as well move into my flat; it was big enough for two and if he gave up his place—well, he could put the money away.

The vague suggestion was that it was to be for somewhere for the pair of us to move into. Marriage wasn't ever mentioned, but it seemed to me that that was what he meant. And I found that as well as paying for the rent on the flat, I was also paying for most of the other bills as well. But I didn't mind! I was happy; I'd found the man of my dreams.'

Alex was frowning. 'In the middle of this happiness you still managed to keep up with your work?' A good question.

'Yes, I did. And, to be fair, Dennis encouraged me. He was working hard himself; we both had to do the same. His work often took him away to conferences and so on. A surprising number of conferences. Every time he went I asked if I could go with him. And always the same answer. He didn't want to be away from me. But he had to learn. It would be better if he went alone.'

'I can guess the end of the story,' Alex said. 'How did you find out?'

She shrugged. 'Quite by accident. He thought so little of me that he hadn't tried very hard to disguise what he was doing. He was away on the West Coast on a conference when a letter came for him marked urgent. I went to his department to ask if they knew exactly where he was; he might need to answer the letter at once. No one seemed to know much about this conference; I guess I got the run-around. I thought I heard a couple of laughs when I asked, but I thought nothing of it. And then, eventually, I got some kind of answer. From a secretary. I thought at the time that she was a bit stand-offish, but since then—I've wondered if she knew what she was doing and did it out of sympathy.'

She had known that some day she would have to tell Alex about this. And she had been dreading it. But now that she had started…surprisingly it seemed quite easy.

'So I phoned the number. A woman's voice answered. A pleasant young voice. "The Clarkson house." House? I thought I was phoning a conference centre. Still, "I'm trying to get in touch with Dr Dennis Clarkson," I said. "Is he there?" "Not at present. My husband has taken the kids down to the beach. May I ask who is calling?" So I told her. "I'm Carly Sinclair. The woman he lives with in Chicago. The woman who thought he was going to marry her." And I rang off.'

Silence. Then, 'Did he ring back?'

'He rang that afternoon and he was furious. He blamed me! He said I'd upset his wife, ruined his vacation, who did I think I was? When I said I thought that I was the woman he loved, he said he did love me. Everything had been a pleasant game. And now look at the trouble he was in!'

'Did you ever see him again?'

'I put all his belongings into black sacks, had them delivered to a storage depot. Then I posted the receipt to his department, with a letter saying that if ever he tried to get in touch again I would make an official complaint against him alleging harassment. And I never heard from him or saw him again.'

He wrapped his arm round her, pulled her to him. 'My poor Carly,' he said. 'Few things are harder to lose than illusions.'

Almost absent-mindedly, she kissed him on the cheek. 'There's more to the story,' she said. 'Perhaps the most important part. The other day I found a picture of him and tore it up. Now I realise it wasn't necessary. I'm over Dennis now. I've met another man. I can see Dennis for what he was. I don't hate him any more; I feel rather sad for him. Alex, I'm strong again.'

'That is good,' he said.

CHAPTER NINE

CARLY still intended Alex to stay the night. In spite of his objections, she made herself a bed on the couch, insisted that he sleep in her bed. 'Apart from anything else, you're too big for the couch,' she pointed out. 'But I've slept on it before.'

'Why don't we sleep together?'

'Because your doctor says no. Alex, I'd love to, but no way would I risk opening that cut. And once in bed together we'd...'

'We could...'

'Whatever you're going to propose, you're wrong. We could not.'

She made them both a milky drink and then went into her bedroom to change into sensible pyjamas and dressing gown. 'We've had a hard day,' she told him, 'and you need your rest. So bed time.'

'Perhaps you're right.' He kissed her on the cheek—the kiss of a brother—and then went to bed. She did feel that something was missing, something wasn't right. But she went to bed herself.

It was comfortable enough on the couch but she just couldn't sleep. Why not? She was certainly tired. She thought of the day that had just passed, the excitement of the evening. It certainly had been exciting.

It was hard having him sleep so close, not being in bed with her. But she was acting as his friend, or even better, acting as his doctor. It was a good idea for him to sleep alone after what had happened to him.

Her thoughts jumped to the other frightening thing that had occurred. She had told Alex about Dennis. She had hated revealing her foolishness to him. But she had done so and he had been understanding, non-judgemental. She had to admit it, she felt better for telling him. No one else knew the story, not her mother, her brothers. She had kept it from them. Why had she told Alex?

He had made her feel better.

She squinted at the red figures on the clock she had placed by the couch. So late and she still hadn't slept. Well, that suggested she probably wouldn't sleep at all.

The decision wasn't taken consciously; it just seemed to happen. She wriggled out of bed. For a moment she stood there irresolute, then deliberately slipped off her pyjamas. There was to be no doubt as to what she was doing.

She walked into the bedroom and he was awake at once. Perhaps he hadn't been able to sleep either. 'Carly?'

'I just want to be with you. I just want us to be together. Nothing more.'

She had lifted the duvet, slid in beside him. The bed was warm; it felt inexpressibly comforting. But exciting too. She felt him ease himself sideways, reach out and touch her naked breasts. A shiver of anticipation shook her.

His voice was hoarse. 'I'm not sure this is a good idea.'

She smiled in the darkness. 'I'm absolutely certain that it is one.'

She bent down to him, gave him a kiss that seemed to drain her soul. And as she felt his need for her, she felt the ache in her breasts, a torment that soon would be eased. Then it all seemed so simple, so straightforward. Somehow she knew what he wanted; it gave her so much pleasure to give it to him. And he could read her too; there was a connection between them that went beyond the physical.

There was no hurry. The desperation of previous times wasn't needed. Slowly, sensually, inevitably they moved towards a shared climax. It was giving and taking, it fused them in a little world of togetherness in which there was nothing but good and no one but the two of them to share it.

'*Ya tebya lyublyu*,' she gasped out at that most sublime of moments. Russian words he had used to her. I love you. She had remembered them, treasured them, and now she used them when they were meant to be used.

She didn't notice the way his body momentarily tensed.

* * *

Ya tebya lyublyu. I love you. Carly lay by Alex's side, holding his hand. *Ya tebya lyublyu.* She had remembered the words. And it was obvious that she did love him. What was he going to do now?

He had to go back to run the hospital at Nyrova. It was the work he had chosen to do, the work that Irina had bequeathed to him. Even though he knew she would have intended no such thing. But he felt she had left him a job to do and it would be betraying her memory if he did not do it.

Just for a moment he thought of Irina and Carly together. Would they have got on? They were radically different, both in appearance and in character. But he thought that ultimately they would have liked each other. They both had the same sense of dedication.

Back to the hospital at Nyrova. Now, for the first time in years, he thought that perhaps there could be an end to his self-imposed task. MedAsia had said that it would like to provide the money for a new hospital, train new staff, reorganise the supplies. That would be good. Perhaps in a few years he could return to his previous high-flying medical career. But did he want to?

He thought about Nyrova, he thought about Carly. And one fact became more and more obvious. She could not live there. All her life she had lived in...well, call it civilisation. She didn't speak the language. She would find the locals hard to befriend. She would miss her brothers desperately. And if she had a baby...how would she cope?

It would hurt her; for that matter, it would hurt him. But tomorrow he would have to tell her. This affair could only be temporary; perhaps they should end it at once. She could never be happy in Nyrova and he could never leave it. As simple as that.

He had made a decision. But he still could not sleep.

By now Carly knew him well. She was content that he should be out of bed first, happy to lie in a half sleep, remembering the wonders of the night before. And there was something else. They were both working a late shift that day. No need to get to the hospital before two o'clock. Perhaps they could… A delicious smell of coffee drifted into the bedroom and she stretched and smiled lazily.

But when he brought the coffee into the bedroom, she instantly knew that something was wrong. For a start, he was dressed. No need for that, a towel would have done if he was going to get back into bed. Evidently he was not. He had left off the bloodied shirt, was pulling the lapels of his jacket across his naked chest. And there was his expression. Harsh as it used to be. But also with a hint of regret. What was worrying him?

'I thought you might want to come back to bed with me,' she said.

He handed her a mug of coffee, sat on the bed—quite a way from her, she noticed. 'I did— I do. But it would not be a good thing. Carly, last night you said to me *ya tebya lyublyu.*'

'It means I love you, in Russian,' she informed

him frostily. 'As I'm sure you know. I've said it several times to you. And I've said it because I meant it. I mean it still. And don't forget, you said it first to me.'

'I know, I remember. And I cannot say that I regret it because, Carly, I meant it too. But it must stop now!'

'Why?' asked Carly, with the calm that comes before a storm.

'Because we cannot live together. And if we love each other, that is what we must want to do. It is not to do with my history. You have made me realise that I must move on with my life, forgive myself, let the past go. For that I thank you. But I must return to Nyrova. And there is no way that you could live there. Carly, listen. Not two hundred miles from the town there was a Gulag—a forced labour camp. There was no need for walls; the countryside kept the prisoners in. And most of them died anyway. That's how harsh a place it is.'

'Living in Nyrova. Don't I have a choice? Aren't I allowed a voice in the matter? It does affect me, you know.'

The old autocratic Alex was back. 'I know that it affects you. But I will spare you the pain of making a choice; I will make it for you. You cannot go. I will not make you unhappy. So the love between us—we must stop it.'

'Is it as easy as that?' she muttered.

'It is not easy; it is hard. Sometimes hard things are necessary.'

If she didn't love him she could hate him, she thought. He was as hard, as implacable, as the land he came from. Well, it wasn't only Russians who could be that way.

'I've got something to show you,' she said sweetly. 'Wait here.'

He looked at her, obviously made uneasy by her change of tone. She stepped out of bed, noted with secret satisfaction the flash of appreciation of her naked body. Then it only took a minute to rummage through the albums in the bottom drawer of her desk. She found the photographs she wanted almost at once and went back to the bedroom.

'You told me of your family, Alex. Now I'm

going to tell you a little about mine.' She handed him a photograph. 'That's a picture of my grandfather.'

He looked at the picture. A burly man with a heavy beard, dressed in the uniform of the Merchant Navy. He could see nothing of Carly's delicate features. But perhaps there was something in the set of the shoulders, the stern gaze, that suggested Carly's character.

'Why am I looking at this?'

She handed him another picture, this time of a battered merchant ship. 'My great-grandfather was First Mate on that ship. The ship was sunk by German dive bombers when she was on her way to Russia in 1943. You've heard of the Arctic Convoys, Alex?'

He shook his head sadly. 'I have indeed. Your grandfather was a brave man.'

'He was, but he was more than that. His ship was sunk at night; he went overboard and was in the water for…well, he would never tell us. All we know was that he was one of only three men who survived. The other fifteen picked up were dead of hypothermia. They froze to death. Alex, that man didn't die because he chose not to. That's the kind of family I'm from. We can take hardship.'

'I see,' he said. 'Yes, I can believe it. So where do we go now?'

'You've got another eight weeks here. We stay lovers, we see what happens. Alex, you said that there could be no future for us; in effect you suggested we should part now. Do you think you can keep away from me over the next few weeks?'

'No,' he said. 'Carly, you do know I'm trying to do the best for you, don't you?'

'I do know. And it's because you love me.'

For the moment there didn't seem to be anything more that they could say to each other. There was a feeling of incompleteness, of decisions put off because they were too harsh or too painful. She was almost pleased when her phone rang. Something else to think about. Just so long as it wasn't another salesman.

It was John Bennett. 'Apart from work, have you got anything personal that you just have to do next week?'

It was an effort to wrench her thoughts from Alex to answer John's simple question. 'Nothing special. I usually drop in to see Jack and Toby and their families.'

'Good. There's a week's intensive course on in London on new microsurgery techniques for neo-nates. It was vastly oversubscribed but I've just learned that someone has dropped out and I've grabbed the spare place. Carly, going would be good for you and the department. D'you want the place?'

'Don't I just. But my work…'

'I can cover that for you. Can you be ready?'

'Watch me,' she said.

She put down her phone and turned to Alex. 'I'm going to London on a course for a week,' she said.

He thought about this. 'This is probably good. Perhaps it would be best for both of us if we had a little time apart. But I will miss you, Carly.'

'Don't think I'm giving up on you,' she said.

It was a good course and when John had said that it was intensive he had been entirely correct.

There were lectures, workshops, texts to study and answer questions on. Carly found it tiring but stimulating. She was learning things that would be useful, would help to save lives. And, since she was exhausted when her head hit the pillow at night, she didn't think of Alex. For a while that was a good thing; her thoughts were still confused. They had decided not to keep in touch by phone; they needed a period of settling down. The course had come at a good time for her.

On the train home, she realised that going on this course had taught her something more than just medicine. She had also learned something about herself. Away from Alex she realised her lack of confidence over the past few years had now disappeared. She wasn't frightened of relationships any more. She and Alex…well, who knew what might come of it? One thing was certain, she was confident, and if necessary she was going to fight.

There was a surprise for her as her train drew into the station. Her brother Jack was waiting to meet her. It wasn't necessary; she could have taken a taxi, but it was good to be met.

Or was there any bad news? He wasn't smiling as he walked towards her along the platform.

'Everything all right, family all doing well?' she asked as he kissed her cheek, picked up her bag.

'The family is fine,' he said. 'Don't worry. Come on, we'll talk in the car.'

Now she was nervous, but she knew she'd have to wait. They got in the car, swung out of the station and into the first traffic queue. 'So what is it, why aren't you smiling?' she asked. 'What have we got to talk about?'

The news he gave her could hardly have been worse. 'Alex Braikovitch flew back to Russia yesterday. He won't be coming back to the hospital here.'

At first she could hardly speak. The enormity of it was just too great. She had plans to get back to her flat, phone him and invite him for dinner or a meal out with her. She knew he'd be interested in the course she had been on. She knew he'd want just to be with her.

'But why?' she burst out eventually. 'He had several weeks left here. He was enjoying himself, enjoying the teaching. And I thought he… Why has he gone back?'

Jack's voice was flat. 'Apparently problems at his hospital. They've got yet another epidemic out there, both the doctors left there are ill and the replacement for Alex just can't cope. There's no chance of anyone local stepping in. Alex is needed desperately. So he's gone.'

'But I was expecting…we were…'

Jack's voice softened. 'I spent a couple of hours talking to him last night. When he told me exactly what it was like in his hospital—well, I'd have done the same in his situation. I told you before, he's a driven man, Carly.'

Her voice was dull. 'I know you did.'

They drove on for a while, found their way on to a main road. 'You were getting quite close to him, weren't you?' Jack asked.

'Quite close. In fact, very close. There were problems, of course. I was scared and he was wary. And he never stopped telling me that eventually he would have to go back to his hospital and I just wouldn't fit in there.'

'He's probably right there. He was thinking of you, Carly.'

'I can think for myself! So he just went. Didn't even try to phone me.' Now, that seemed to be the last betrayal.

'I tried to talk him into phoning you. He said there was no point; it would only cause you pain and he thought a clean break would be the best. The sad thing is, it was obvious that he desperately wanted to talk to you.'

'So why didn't he?'

'You know what he's like. Better than me, I suppose. Once he's decided that something is the right thing to do, then he'll do it, whatever the cost.'

Jack pointed to the glove compartment. 'He didn't leave without a word. There's a letter there for you.'

She opened the compartment, took out the letter. An expensive white envelope. 'Carly

Sinclair' written on it in broad pen-strokes. His writing was like his character—clear, bold, definite. She put the envelope in her pocket; she would open it later, in private.

'Want to come back home for supper?' Jack asked. 'Have a family chat with Miranda, play with your niece for a while?'

It was tempting; it might even be good for her. But she wanted to be alone with her misery. Read her letter and get angry with him in private. This wasn't fair! Why should she have two lousy love affairs?

'Think I'd like to get back to my place,' she said. 'I'm pretty tired; I need a bath and bed.'

Jack stretched his arm round her, gave her a quick hug. 'Remember you've still got a family that loves you,' he said.

She was like a little child, putting off a treat— or a tragedy. She arrived home, made herself a small meal, had her bath. Then she poured herself a glass of red wine and opened his letter. As she read his words, imploring her to understand why he had to go, how hard it was to leave her, how he felt a clean break was the best for both of them, tears started to threaten. But it wasn't until she got to the end that they fell. For there followed three words in Cyrillic script—she thought she could almost read what they said. But underneath there was a translation.

In case you cannot read this, or guess it, it says, 'I love you.'
Alex.

She read the letter twice more, blotting off her tears as they dropped on to the paper.

'I certainly didn't want him to go,' John Bennett said to her as she sat in his room the following Monday morning. 'He did try to find out if someone else could take his place, but it wasn't possible. It's such a shame. His lectures were superb and so was the work he was doing. Though I can understand his reasons for going.'

'So everyone says,' Carly agreed, her voice betraying none of the emotion churning inside her. 'He was a good doctor. He'll be missed— by all sorts of people.'

'I offered him the chance to come back. I said any time, let me know when you can come and I'll be in touch with MedAsia and see what we can arrange. He said that he very much doubted if he'd be able to come back. There was work ahead as far as he could see. But that he had learned much in his stay here and had been made to feel very welcome. He wanted everyone to know that the people of his home town would benefit tremendously from what he had picked up here.'

'Great,' said Carly. 'A pity he couldn't have stayed longer. He might have learned more.'

'True.' John steepled his hands. 'I take it that you and Alex have become quite close.'

'We work well together,' she said.

John nodded. 'It's a pity that he's based so far away.'

'Well, it does mean that working together is a bit difficult.'

'Indeed,' said John. 'Now, tell me about the course.'

CHAPTER TEN

ALEX put his hands to the small of his back, tried to lean backwards. Stiffened muscles pained him as he stretched them. He had been bent over an operating table all morning; it wasn't the most comfortable of positions. In fact his life over the past month hadn't been all that comfortable. Working a regular twelve plus hour day, seven days a week. Not a recipe for an easy life.

But now perhaps things might ease a little. He was getting an extra doctor. He'd been told a competent, experienced doctor. Just what he needed. With three doctors on site, perhaps he could settle down to a ten-hour day and even have the occasional day off.

If he was honest with himself, he would have

to admit that he was glad that the work had been so exhausting. It had been a month since he had left England, left Carly. And every spare minute he had, he thought of her. Not that he had many spare minutes. He knew he had made the right decision. But it had been hard.

He'd asked her not to write to him in the letter he'd left for her, and had wondered if she'd ignore him. Part of him hoped so. There'd been moments when he'd been desperate to hear from her. And more than once he had taken pen and paper, wondered if he could write to her—just to tell her how he was getting on. Nothing wrong with writing, was there?

Yes, there was. It prolonged a relationship that had to die.

He shivered as snow eddied round him. He was standing in the shelter of a hut that stood on the side of the Nyrova airstrip. A gang of men in front of him had just swept the thick of the snow off the runway, were now waiting to man-handle the cargo of medical supplies into the hut. Alex usually liked to watch the supplies being delivered, make sure that nothing had been missed. And he was also here to welcome his new doctor. He knew very little about his new colleague and just hoped he was used to bad weather; after today there'd be no chance of flying out. They could look forward to three months of bitter winter.

Winter. Just what I need, Alex thought.

He heard a humming noise somewhere, searched the snow-darkened sky until he saw the little transport plane heading low across the plains. It grew quickly larger; the humming noise turned into a rattle and then an ear-splitting roar. Sometimes Alex wondered just how much longer the plane would be airworthy.

Nearly here. The plane touched down just past the hut, bounced once and then slowed to a near stop. It turned, taxied back to park near the hut. The gang hurried forward to unload from the freight hold. And the pilot climbed out of the cockpit, down the little ladder and then turned to help his passenger down. A slight figure, well wrapped in a thick coat and hat. Necessary in this weather.

Alex ran forward to greet his new doctor. He hoped the man would be happy here; he'd been honest about the conditions and…

The man had stopped, was waiting for Alex to come to him. Alex held out his hand, peered at the face under the hat and… 'Carly?'

It just couldn't be!

'Dr Sinclair,' she said, shaking his hand, which was still outstretched in shock. 'I've been sent by MedAsia to help you for the next three months. How are you, Alex?'

First he was dumbfounded. Second, he was just about to get angry. People didn't play silly games like this on him. 'What are you doing here?'

'You wanted an experienced doctor, you've got one. Me. And I'll cost you nothing; MedAsia is paying all my fees and expenses.'

'You're here for three months! It's ridiculous; you'll never last.'

'Alex! I thought we'd taught you that you don't talk to your staff like that. And you don't think that you're always automatically right. What changed you back to the way you were?'

'Sheer frustration. Carly, you don't know what it's been like being here on my own. After being with you. But you're here! And this is the way I've greeted you!'

It struck him that he hadn't been the most welcoming of lovers. But then the shock had been so great. 'Carly, I just can't… What made you…? How are you?'

'At the moment I appear to be freezing to death. Aren't you pleased to see me, Alex?'

He could tell by her smile that she was teasing him. 'It's not like me not to know what I'm feeling,' he muttered. 'But Carly…I just can't tell you how I feel.'

'I think that's good,' she said. 'And, if it's any consolation, for the past week I've been wondering how I'd feel when I saw you for the first time. Well, now I know. I'm glad. Ever so glad.'

He took her two hands, led her to the door of the hut. At the doorway he turned and called to the men to bring the doctor's cases straight over.

The hut door slammed shut; perhaps it was a little warmer inside. And the wind had gone. He took off her hat, stripped off his own gloves, then reached out to touch her cheeks.

'You ask me if I'm pleased to see you. Carly, I've dreamed about you every night. The thought of you has kept me working in the day, the memories of what we did together have been the things that made my life worth living.'

'And I've thought of you, Alex, thought of you so much. Sometimes I've been blazingly angry at you for leaving me... No, don't tell me. I know you had to go and I sympathise. Anyway, it's worked out. You had to come here. I had to follow you. You can kiss me now.'

So he kissed her. 'When I kiss you,' he said, 'it's like coming home. It's where I belong, where I want, where I need to be.'

Her eyes sparkled at his words. 'That's lovely. And it's true.'

Then there was a jolt of common sense; he had to think of reality. 'Carly, I spent so much time telling you. Life here is hard! This is nothing like...'

She silenced him with a finger on his lips. 'Life

here will be easy because I'll be with you,' she said with a smile. 'I've even earned a few words of Russian. *Ya tebya lyublyu.*'

He looked into her eyes and saw nothing but love and hope for the future. Their future. Together. '*Ya tebya lyublyu,*' he murmured, kissing her as if he'd never stop. '*Ya tebya lyublyu.* My Carly. My love.'

EPILOGUE

IT HAD been a year. Carly felt odd coming home. No, not exactly coming home—she had two homes now. One was here in northern England, one was in a distant desolate part of Russia. She was at home in both, happy in both.

For a while life in Russia had been hard. There was the weather, a different kind of medicine to practise, the loneliness. But she had managed. If it was cold, she wrapped up. She had got to know people, had been accepted by them. Now she could speak a moderate amount of Russian— though she must be one of the few people who started learning a foreign language by memorising a hundred medical terms.

And how could she really be lonely when she had Alex? That made up for everything.

The train was running through a deep cutting now; soon they would be in the station. This was a journey she had made a hundred times before. She stretched out her hands to Alex, her husband. He was sitting contentedly opposite her, nursing their two-month-old son. Alex was never happier than when holding his child.

Being a father seemed in some ways to have mellowed him. He was still the tough administrator, able to take hard decisions when necessary. But he was calmer, less abrasive. He was at peace with himself.

'I'll put him in his carry-cot,' she said. 'We'll be there in five minutes.'

As always, Alex was reluctant to let go of his son. He kissed him on the forehead before handing him over. There was a small squeak as the baby was tucked in. 'Now then, Sergei Jack,' she said fondly, stroking his cheek, 'you have to behave. You're going to meet all your relations. You're lucky having so many cousins.' So Sergei Jack went instantly to sleep. He was a good child.

They had decided together, had given him

names from two cultures. He was going to be brought up speaking two languages. Perhaps when he was a man he might… Carly shook her head. Time would tell what might happen to him. She was content to wait.

She smiled at her husband, who smiled back. 'You've got that expression on your face that means you're thinking something,' he said. 'Tell me what it is.'

'I was remembering Sergei's birth. You, the cool man, always keeping his emotions under control. You were told to leave the Delivery Room for a while, told by your own midwife! You were getting too excited.'

'I was excited.' He was obviously quite happy about it.

'And when you came back in and the baby was born, you lifted him up to Heaven and shouted, *ti takaya krasivaya*. Just as you did the first time I met you. You know, I might have started loving you that minute.'

'It didn't take that long for me,' he said, giving her a kiss.

* * *

They were met by her big brother Jack. She looked along the platform, saw him striding towards them. It was so good to see that craggy face again. He had been—still was—a good brother to her. As best he could, he had kept a cautious eye on her and on her twin Toby. Now, she knew that some of their decisions might have caused him to worry. It was marvellous how having a child of your own made you sympathetic to others' feelings.

'So how's my little sister?' A kiss, a big hug. Then he turned to Alex and the two men hugged each other. It always surprised Carly to see how readily Alex hugged people. But now she hugged people too. Still the sight of two of the most important men in her life hugging each other made her a little tearful. But so happy.

Jack bent over the carry-cot, peered at the tiny face. 'I don't know if he's going to look like a Braikovitch or a Sinclair. But he's a gorgeous little lad. Come on, the rest of the family is anxious to meet you; this is the first time we've all got together. You're not too tired after the journey?'

Carly shook her head. 'We had a good night's

sleep in the airport hotel. We're fine and we want to see everybody. Let's go.'

They were to meet at Jack's house. And the rest of the family were there together. Jack's wife Miranda, with baby Esme—who was now so much bigger. Toby and Annie, with Charlie and Lara. There were four babies. So there had to be a photograph of four small figures huddled together on a couch. 'Not a lot of teeth about, are there?' Toby joked. And afterwards there were presents, and photographs to look at, other people's babies to hold and all the necessary gossip to catch up on.

It had only taken two months before Alex had asked her to marry him. She knew he would have asked before, but he'd felt he had to let her find out if she could survive in his town. She had done more than survive. Quickly, she'd come to like it.

They'd decided to marry at once. Jack had been the only relation who could fly out, to give her away. Carly had asked if they could be married in the same church where Alex's wife and child were buried. They could, and the service had been wonderful. But the English half of the family were not to be done out of a wedding, so they were going to have a service of celebration, held by the Reverend Madeleine Hall, the Dell Owen Hospital chaplain. Carly and Miranda and Annie had been planning it for months, by post.

Carly looked at her brothers. She remembered them as the three of them had been just two and a half years ago. Unmarried, uncertain, their futures in doubt. For the first time in a while she remembered their half-joking nickname—The Good, the Bad and the Ugly. It wasn't deserved now. Toby wasn't bad—not that he ever had been. But now no one could be more devoted to his wife and family—except perhaps Jack. Jack wasn't ugly. He still had a stern face—but he seemed to smile much more now. He had a lot to smile about.

And herself. The Good? She'd spread her wings. She'd flown to Russia, chased after the man she loved, married him. Was that good?

She smiled. It was.

MEDICAL™

 *Large Print*

Titles for the next six months…

January

SINGLE DAD, OUTBACK WIFE	Amy Andrews
A WEDDING IN THE VILLAGE	Abigail Gordon
IN HIS ANGEL'S ARMS	Lynne Marshall
THE FRENCH DOCTOR'S MIDWIFE BRIDE	Fiona Lowe
A FATHER FOR HER SON	Rebecca Lang
THE SURGEON'S MARRIAGE PROPOSAL	Molly Evans

February

THE ITALIAN GP'S BRIDE	Kate Hardy
THE CONSULTANT'S ITALIAN KNIGHT	Maggie Kingsley
HER MAN OF HONOUR	Melanie Milburne
ONE SPECIAL NIGHT…	Margaret McDonagh
THE DOCTOR'S PREGNANCY SECRET	Leah Martyn
BRIDE FOR A SINGLE DAD	Laura Iding

March

THE SINGLE DAD'S MARRIAGE WISH	Carol Marinelli
THE PLAYBOY DOCTOR'S PROPOSAL	Alison Roberts
THE CONSULTANT'S SURPRISE CHILD	Joanna Neil
DR FERRERO'S BABY SECRET	Jennifer Taylor
THEIR VERY SPECIAL CHILD	Dianne Drake
THE SURGEON'S RUNAWAY BRIDE	Olivia Gates

MILLS & BOON®
Pure reading pleasure

1207 LP 2P P1 Medical

MEDICAL™

Large Print

April

THE ITALIAN COUNT'S BABY	Amy Andrews
THE NURSE HE'S BEEN WAITING FOR	Meredith Webber
HIS LONG-AWAITED BRIDE	Jessica Matthews
A WOMAN TO BELONG TO	Fiona Lowe
WEDDING AT PELICAN BEACH	Emily Forbes
DR CAMPBELL'S SECRET SON	Anne Fraser

May

THE MAGIC OF CHRISTMAS	Sarah Morgan
THEIR LOST-AND-FOUND FAMILY	Marion Lennox
CHRISTMAS BRIDE-TO-BE	Alison Roberts
HIS CHRISTMAS PROPOSAL	Lucy Clark
BABY: FOUND AT CHRISTMAS	Laura Iding
THE DOCTOR'S PREGNANCY BOMBSHELL	Janice Lynn

June

CHRISTMAS EVE BABY	Caroline Anderson
LONG-LOST SON: BRAND-NEW FAMILY	Lilian Darcy
THEIR LITTLE CHRISTMAS MIRACLE	Jennifer Taylor
TWINS FOR A CHRISTMAS BRIDE	Josie Metcalfe
THE DOCTOR'S VERY SPECIAL CHRISTMAS	Kate Hardy
A PREGNANT NURSE'S CHRISTMAS WISH	Meredith Webber

MILLS & BOON®
Pure reading pleasure

1207 LP 2P P2 Medical